UNHINGED

GARY McCARRAGHER

Unhinged, Published November, 2013

Editorial and Proofreading Services: Shannon Miller and Karen Grennan

Interior Layout and Cover Design: Howard Communigrafix, Inc.

Cover Image: iStockphoto by Getty Images; ImagineGolf; Vetta Stock Photo, file #2298811

Author Photo: Susan McCarragher

 **SDP Publishing**

Published by SDP Publishing, an imprint of SDP Publishing Solutions, LLC.

For more information about this book contact Lisa Akoury-Ross by email at lross@SDPPublishing.com.

ISBN-13 (print): 978-0-9889381-1-3

eISBN-13 (ebook): 978-0-9889381-2-0

Library of Congress Control Number: 2013936867

Dedication

To Erin, James, and Susan

Acknowledgments

I would like to thank Beverly Swerling, Linda M. DeVore, Laurie Rosen, and Doris Bloodsworth for their valuable assistance. I'm grateful to Susan McCarragher for her suggestions and encouragement, and to W. H. Schroeder for his expert technical assistance. I'd especially like to thank my editors, Shannon Miller and Karen Grennan, for their fine work, and my publisher, Lisa Akoury-Ross, for her expert guidance and support.

The struggle itself toward the heights is enough to fill a man's heart. One must imagine Sisyphus happy.

Albert Camus
The Myth of Sisyphus

UNHINGED

Prologue

August 2005

Dr. Richard Chase burst through the front doors of the Black Diamond Tennis Club into the sweltering evening. He had to get away, far away. Where? He didn't know, and he didn't care. He ran, frantically searching for his SUV, his jangling keys nearly jumping out of his pocket.

Richard jabbed his key into the lock and threw himself behind the wheel. The DVD, the one that had caused him such humiliation and now threatened to jeopardize his career, burned like fire in his brain. He slammed the car into reverse and stomped on the gas.

The sickening thud of metal on flesh stopped him cold. He sprang out of the vehicle and slumped to the ground.

Oh God, no! Please, no.

Four months earlier

With the brilliant sun of a New England spring morning beaming into his study at home, Dr. Richard Chase admired the blueprints spread out before him on his large oak desk.

Magnificent!

After countless revisions, Richard had finally found the perfect design for his state-of-the-art, ten thousand-square-foot Gastroenterology Endoscopy Center. He smiled lovingly, the smile of a new father gazing into the eyes of his firstborn.

He peered out his window into the beautiful grove of elm trees on his property. A muffled ring came from under the Sunday *Boston Globe* on the computer table.

"Hello?"

"Hey Richard, it's Tom. Mr. McAllister just called me. He'd like to see you at noon, at his place."

"When, *today?*"

"Yep."

"Did he say why?"

"Nope. Will you be able to make it?"

Richard hesitated. "Ah yes, of course. Tell him I'll be there at noon, sharp."

"Great. I'll—"

"Did he sound okay? I mean, he's not upset about something, is he?"

"He didn't sound upset."

"Good. Listen, I think we've finally got it. The layout is sensational."

"Glad to hear it. I'll let him know."

Richard ended the call and chuckled. Wasn't this typical McAllister? Despite his advanced age of eighty-three, he exuded such energy, such passion for his ongoing projects.

Over thirty years my senior and he can still work me under the table.

Evidently, the old boy couldn't wait to see the latest revisions. Oh yes, today was going to be special. Richard could feel it in his bones.

A light knock came at the open door.

"Who were you talking to, sweetheart?"

Richard swung around to find his wife, Leslie, standing in the doorway. Rings of tightly curled blond hair poured around her heart-shaped face. She had changed out of her painter's outfit—faded yellow capris and an old, white cotton blouse with a collage of paint streaks—and was wearing a lavender silk bathrobe he had given her for her birthday.

He approached her, smiling. "Tom Waller. Says McAllister wants to see me this morning. I think he wants to see the new blueprints."

Leslie tucked away coils of her unruly hair. "Now? On a Sunday morning?"

He shrugged. "I guess he's anxious to get going. You know how excited he is about this."

He rested his hands on her slender waist. "You don't mind, do you, Les? I won't be long."

"Well I did have other plans for us." Leslie stood up on her toes and gave her husband a wet, open-mouthed kiss on his full lips. "I can't stop thinking about our roll on the carpet last night. Besides, who does he think he is, expecting you to drop everything and come running at a moment's notice? You deserve better than that. He makes me so damned mad."

"I can tell," he said, grinning. He pulled her tightly toward him. "He's just a bit impatient. That's all. Don't forget, he is giving me five million bucks."

"With a lot of strings."

Leslie tugged on the silk belt fastening her robe and wriggled her shoulders. The bathrobe fell to the floor, exposing a matching lavender chemise barely covering her full breasts. She caressed his face, sliding her delicate fingers over his salt and pepper stubble down to his strong, square jaw.

"Anyway, I don't care if that pompous ass is giving you the moon. Look what you're doing, sweetheart—running out on a Sunday morning like his obedient slave."

"Don't be ridiculous," he said, kissing her neck. "I'm nobody's slave."

She stroked his broad, well-defined chest.

"Why don't you call him back and tell him you can see him later?" She slid her pelvis over his muscular thigh and ran her fingers through his thick, brown hair. "We're in luck. Justin is still sleeping."

Richard took her hand and led her up the stairs. As they entered the bedroom, he caressed her silky smooth back.

"I'll tell His Majesty I was unexpectedly detained."

They laughed and fell onto the bed.

—⚍—

Richard showered, shaved, and threw on a pair of khakis and a black golf shirt. On his way out, he stopped at the partly opened door to the basement. A recording of Bach's *Goldberg Variations* played on guitar, filtered up to him. He walked down several steps.

"Les? I'm leaving now. Honey?"

Leslie looked up from her canvas and smiled. "Okay, dear. Just be careful. Say 'hi' to the pompous ass for me."

Richard returned a grateful smile, sprang up the stairs, and flew out the front door.

Richard sped along the pothole-laden freeway in his classic '72 Jaguar through the Berkshires. McAllister's estate in Westchase was forty-five minutes from Richard's home in Cambridge. He glanced at the blueprints next to him on the passenger seat. His stomach churned with excitement. He wished Leslie could be more accepting of McAllister, but at least for now, he wasn't going to let it bother him. She'd warm up to the old man. Perhaps they should invite him over for dinner.

Richard smiled and shook his head in amazement, still flabbergasted at the whirlwind series of events that brought him to this miraculous opportunity. If not for McAllister's life-threatening illness seven months earlier, they would never have met, and none of these marvelous developments would have unfolded. Funny how great things can sometimes rise out of near tragedy.

McAllister had presented to the emergency room with severe abdominal pain, high fever, and jaundice. An emergency room physician had told the family that McAllister had a severe gallbladder attack with a blocked bile duct and severe infection in the bloodstream.

After consulting with the ER staff, the primary care

physician, and the CEO of the hospital, McAllister's oldest son, Jonathon, insisted on obtaining the services of Dr. Richard Chase, renowned for his expertise in complicated biliary and pancreatic endoscopy. And so, Dr. Chase, who happened to not be on call, was summoned out of his bed on a cold, pre-dawn Sunday morning late last September to evaluate the seriously ill patient. Richard knew the competent gastroenterologist on call could have handled the case. Leslie had pleaded for him to refuse the request. But that overwhelming tug of excitement and responsibility rushed through him. Before Leslie could further protest, he was on his way.

The procedure was routine and performed by most gastroenterologists. However, given the patient's advanced age, unstable condition, and the added risk that comes with working on a high-profile patient such as the venerable James P. McAllister, the case was anything but routine.

Richard was well aware of a similar case in the city less than a month earlier that had ended in cardiac arrest on the table. As celebrated as his record was, he knew that he wasn't immune to such catastrophes. Nobody was.

Two difficult hours later, Richard had cleared the bile duct of multiple large stones, paving the way for gallbladder removal by the general surgeon, Dr. Christopher Taylor. Taylor congratulated Richard for a heroic effort and a grand success. Richard shrugged it off as routine, but inside he felt a particular pride in his work that morning.

Three days later, the grateful patient went home, much to the jubilation of his family. The next day, a small article appeared in the Metro section of the *Boston Globe* detailing the prominent J.P. McAllister's life-threatening illness and the life-saving intervention by Dr. Richard Chase and Dr. Christopher Taylor.

At the old man's insistence, the McAllister residence threw a gala party to honor Drs. Chase and Taylor about a month after McAllister's hospital discharge. The guest list consisted of the rich and famous of the Boston business world and social scene. McAllister gave a heartfelt speech, thanking his two men of medicine, especially the "great Dr. Chase," for giving the wealthy patriarch a little more precious time with his family and friends before going to his maker. Even Taylor made it perfectly clear—the eminent Dr. Chase was the star of the show.

Richard had felt embarrassed about that evening of lavish recognition. He was grateful that no physicians other than McAllister's primary care doctor had been invited. On the other hand, in a profession where excellence is increasingly taken for granted, and criticism—often unfounded—is hastily delivered at every opportunity, Richard couldn't deny that McAllister's act of gratitude had felt good.

Then came that fateful day two weeks later. Richard innocently commented to McAllister during a routine office follow-up that he hoped one day to free himself from the frustrating inefficiency and lack of control unavoidable with hospital practice. He shared his dream of building his own freestanding endoscopy center on a beautiful, four-acre parcel of land he had purchased five years ago in Cambridge.

Richard had made the same comment to other patients and doctors during the last three years since he first conceived the dream. About a year ago, he had actually begun planning the project. Then he woke up one morning to find his seven-thousand shares of pharmaceutical stock had become worthless after people began dropping dead from a medication made by the company. That catastrophe had killed his dream for the foreseeable future, but he hadn't stopped thinking and talking about the center, especially when hospital problems arose.

To Richard's best recollection, McAllister hadn't responded to the comment. Richard had all but forgotten his remarks until a month later, when he received an invitation from McAllister to visit his estate early one evening.

McAllister made an unbelievable offer—a five million dollar gift to build a state-of-the-art endoscopy center on Richard's land. No expense would be spared. An additional interest-free loan of any amount was available, if required, to completely fund the first year's operations.

There were conditions. McAllister required that the facility be named the McAllister Institute for Endoscopy. In addition, he insisted that the family corporation retain fifty-one percent ownership of the land, real estate, and hard assets, and be a fifty-one percent shareholder. Richard would be awarded forty-nine percent ownership and shares. In addition, he would assume the position of CEO and retain full control of operations—all without one dime of capital investment.

Barely able to contain his joy, Richard had raced home to Leslie with the news. Her eyes widened and her jaw fell open. But then to his surprise, she frowned and shook her head.

"Are you sure this is kosher? It sounds a bit fishy."

"What do you mean, fishy? The old buck appreciates what I did for him. Is that so hard to believe?"

"No, but these filthy-rich business types make me nervous. Isn't he the big newspaper giant? His family's always in the news, buying this and that."

"So what? They're a wealthy family. That's what wealthy families do."

Try as he might, Richard hadn't been able to change her skepticism about getting into bed with such a powerful family. Nonetheless, the plan went forward. The next day, their joint venture, Freedom Medical Corporation, was set up, and five million dollars was made available for immediate use.

Two weeks later, the corporation purchased Richard's parcel of land for a generous price and hired an architect to draw up plans for the endoscopy center. The building would be large enough to accommodate his group of three gastroenterologists, and if all went well, other GI physicians in the city. Richard could not have been more excited and happy.

Four weeks later, McAllister threw a lavish bash at his estate for Richard, his two partners, a dozen other handpicked gastroenterologists, and the usual assortment of wealthy friends who had shown up at the first soirée several months earlier. Richard resisted such pomp and circumstance, and felt especially uncomfortable when McAllister insisted on a formal toast, crowning Richard medical director, CEO, and Lord High Everything. Richard figured, what the hell. He had earned it, hadn't he? Even his competition thought so. As they say, you have to be good to be lucky.

Now three months later, here he was, approaching the imposing wrought-iron gate and high stone wall surrounding McAllister's magnificent property. Richard caught himself smiling into the surveillance camera.

The gates opened slowly. Richard slapped the steering wheel.

Time to get to work.

3

As Richard's car crept through the open gates, he caught a glimpse of McAllister's home, a spectacular three-story, twelve thousand-square foot New England colonial estate, hidden by a grove of mixed hardwoods. He drove onto the narrow, red cobblestone lane, lined on each side by maples that formed a canopy over him. He emerged from the natural tunnel to view a colossal, white marble fountain spouting triple streams of water. He parked his car in front of the house.

A maid escorted Richard into the spacious library, served him coffee with a selection of pastries, and asked him to wait a few minutes. He marveled at the beauty surrounding him— stunning oak floor, ornate bookshelves covering most of the two side walls, cathedral ceiling with a magnificent chandelier at its center—all lit perfectly by diffused light from old brass lamps. He breathed in the odor of old books and wood and smiled. He was suddenly a young medical student in the medical library at Johns Hopkins.

The heavy oak door behind him slammed shut. Richard spun around to see J. P. McAllister approaching him. He was a formidable presence, standing more than six feet tall. His Roman nose and strong jaw balanced his large, wrinkled forehead marked with age spots. Thick, pure-white hair combed straight back fell evenly at his collar and slightly turned up at the ends. He wore a white suit open to the bottom button, a red tie, a white vest from which a gold watch fob hung, and shiny black shoes. He gripped his signature gold-trimmed, wood-and-ebony cane, which he'd once said had been handed down to him from his late father, Andrew Emerson McAllister.

McAllister peered over his perfectly round, black spectacles toward Richard and cleared his throat.

Richard smiled warmly and extended his hand. "Good afternoon, Mr. McAllister. How are you, sir?"

McAllister grabbed his belly and pounded the floor with his cane. "Terrible! Guts all twisted up since last night."

Richard stepped toward his patient, extending an open palm for palpation of his abdomen.

"What? Sir, are you in pain?"

"Worse, much worse."

McAllister waved Richard off and jabbed his cane toward an old, mahogany high-backed chair to Richard's left. "Sit."

Richard eased himself down onto the edge of the chair. The old man was clearly upset, but why? Was he sick? Surely he couldn't be thinking his "twisted guts" had anything to do with the procedure Richard had performed.

McAllister approached his guest, taking short, measured steps. He stopped within a cane's reach of Richard's knees and peered at him over the top of his glasses.

"Young man, look at the wall behind me and tell me what you see."

Richard scanned the wall. "I'm not sure what you mean." He looked at McAllister. "Sir, are you feeling all right?"

McAllister turned sharply and pointed his cane at the wall.

"Look again. What do you see?"

Richard shrugged and shook his head. "Lots of things. Some pictures . . ."

"Most important thing on that wall. Tell me *now*!"

Richard stood up and shook his head. "Sir, would you mind telling me what this is all about?"

McAllister pointed his cane at the area above the entrance, his arm straight as an arrow, and grunted impatiently.

Richard scratched the side of his head. "The *flag*?"

"Yes, my young man, the flag. Hung up that old relic over those doors myself the day we moved in. Bought it in 1948 here in Boston for five dollars. Nothing in here, in this whole house, means a pinch of snuff without *that*. Now I'm curious, what does that five-dollar flag mean to you?"

Richard turned toward McAllister and frowned. An unsettling thought suddenly flashed through his mind.

"What does the flag mean to me?"

"You heard me, young man. Look me straight in the eye and give me an answer."

McAllister removed his gold timepiece from his vest pocket and, without taking his eyes off Richard, expertly snapped open the cover.

"I'll thank you to hurry up. I'm a busy man."

Richard cleared his throat. "Well, it represents the fifty states, unified under one constitution. Our country."

McAllister tapped his cane on the floor and grinned in mock approval. "I see. Anything else?"

Richard turned to his questioner. "Mr. McAllister, with all due respect, why are you asking me this? Is something wrong?"

"Yes! Something is wrong. Since you can't find the words to answer my simple question, I'm going to give you my answer." He pointed to Richard's chair with aggravated jabs of his cane. "Now sit down!"

Richard's back stiffened.

Oh God. Could this be about my political activism?

"My father, Andrew E. McAllister, was born in Scotland, 1890. He came to this great country on an old, dilapidated boat in 1905, sent by his grandparents after his own parents died, to an uncle in New York to make a life in this new, strange country. Started out penniless, but with a little help from his uncle, a razor-sharp mind, and the wonderful opportunity only this great country could give him, he worked his way up the newspaper business until he became one of the three biggest men in the business—despite the Depression."

"Sir, I—"

"Quiet! So there I was, growing up in New York in the '30's. Little rich kid. Had the world on a string. Then came Pearl Harbor. Thousands of men enlisted to answer the call. But not me. Didn't mean a thing to me. I was an eighteen-year-old young buck eager to screw on my fists and reach for the sky. I was the son of the great and powerful Andrew McAllister, already in the family business, being groomed for stardom. No chance I was getting drafted; father would see to it."

McAllister took a deep breath and smacked his cane onto the floor. Richard sat motionless, stone-faced, his mind racing.

"Then one day, he called me into his office and told me to enlist."

Down came the cane, steel tip striking on wood.

"Just like that! I almost wet myself. Asked him—why? What

about the business? I wasn't being drafted. Why did he want me to go? You know what he said, my young man?"

"Sir, I don't—"

"Payback. My wonderful opportunity in life had come from this great country. I couldn't continue to take without giving, he said. As for him, he had already given over ten million dollars to the war effort. I protested. It didn't matter; his mind was made up. I couldn't expect to enjoy the fruits of the American dream without doing my part. Mother and I hated him for it. For weeks, that great woman cried herself to sleep, but in the end, I went off to war. Joined the Marines in early 1942 while the Japs were seizing the Dutch East Indies, Singapore, and Burma. Never forgot the day I left—March 12. He hugged me until I thought my back would break. Tears rolled down his cheeks. First time I ever saw him cry. Pacific Theater, '42 to '45. What a hellhole."

Once again, the cane came crashing down, the solid thud echoing off the walls.

"Midway—American dive bombers attacking, destroying all four carriers. Changed everything. Turned the tide in the Pacific. Put the Jap Imperial Navy on the defensive. Midway and Pearl Harbor were secure. Then came the hellholes *I* was involved in. The battle for Guadalcanal—six long months— Operation Cartwheel, invasion of the Marshall Islands, the Marianas, Guam, the Philippines, and finally, the Battle of Iwo Jima. By Jesus, that MacArthur was a pistol."

McAllister punctuated each battle with a menacing smash of his cane, driving the steel butt of his weapon into the floor.

Richard remained silent and still. Perspiration soaked his face.

"Those sons of bitches with their suicide bombers. But we did it. We defeated them. Almost bought it on Iwo Jima, March of '45. Still got the shrapnel in my back."

McAllister's cheeks reddened. He puffed as if he had just fought off an intruder. With an unmistakable spark in his eyes, he reached around with his free hand and awkwardly punched his left flank. The impact caused him to stumble forward. Richard leapt forward to catch him, but was sharply waved off.

"When I finally got home, I was treated like the second coming. Father shook my hand, called me a hero, told me to be proud and carry my pride for the rest of my days. I'll never forget those words."

McAllister raised his cane toward a large oil painting of his father hanging several feet to the right of the flag.

"My father taught me almost everything I know and helped make me a wealthy man. But the most important thing he gave me had nothing to do with money. Patriotism, love of flag and country, fierce pride to be an American."

He turned toward Richard. "Just thought you should know a little bit about my life and know where I stand on such matters. Now, if you don't mind, young man, I'd like to know where you stand on these things."

Richard felt his face flush.

"Dr. Chase, I've asked you a question."

Richard looked at McAllister and sighed forcefully. He spoke with a deliberate slowness, careful not to raise his voice. "For the record, I also take pride in my American citizenship. I honor and respect the American ideal, our great flag, and everything it stands for. And I deeply appreciate your brave contribution to this country."

McAllister stared expressionless at Richard. "I see. Is that all?"

"Excuse me? Mr. McAllister, I don't understand what you—"

"Call of duty. It troubles me that you failed to mention this. All those beautiful words don't mean a speck of rat shit without a commitment to serve our country. Just empty words. Take the Iraq war, for example.

"Thank goodness we have enough brave, young Americans to answer that call of duty. I'm very proud of their efforts, fighting for democracy and freedom, defending us against those God-forsaken terrorists. They're not just talking; they're risking their lives. What do *you* think?"

The missile had hit its target.

"Word has it you've attended anti-war marches and protests in the city. And such interesting signs: 'Military parents— Think!' 'Soldier—Think!' Takes a dedicated man to walk for miles carrying signs."

Richard flashed back to last summer. He stood rigid, his insides churning. The terrible realization now shot through Richard with a jolt. A frightful concoction of shock, bewilderment, indignation, anger, and fear came rushing forth. The possibility of such a catastrophic loss, of having his dream snatched from under his nose and irrevocably snuffed out as quickly as a bullet could destroy a life, were unimaginable. Richard couldn't feel his legs. A flush of perspiration shot through his pores.

"Look, I don't know what you've heard, but—" He looked directly into McAllister's eyes and gritted his teeth. "Yes, I attended marches—to stop the needless killing of our soldiers and innocent civilians."

McAllister produced a crumpled paper from his pocket. "Impressive resume we have here. Active member in Worldwide Physicians Against War."

"Mr. McAllister, please let me—"

McAllister scoffed. "Please let you what? Set me straight? You'll get your chance." He pulled out another piece of paper, slowly unfolded it, adjusted his glasses, and cleared his throat.

"Quite the philanthropist as well, it seems. I see you gave ten thousand dollars to the WPAW. Think back now. Remember?"

Richard groaned. "Sir, if you'll just give me a chance to explain."

Down crashed the cane onto the floor. "I said you'd get your chance!"

McAllister again reached into his jacket, pulled out yet another piece of paper, snapped it open with a wave in the air, and cleared his throat, this time with particular force.

> "Furthermore, I have grave concerns, not only with our leaders, but also with many others in the military who support this action.
>
> The model soldier is, among other things, defined as one who answers the call with absolute, unconditional obedience, as if the request were not from an elected representative, but an edict from an emperor. Such a response, however, eliminates the need for military leadership to be rigorously accountable. While strict obedience and discipline are certainly necessary for an effective military, I believe this approach, when taken to the extreme, is frightfully dangerous and a threat to our democracy."

McAllister read on, punctuating the points that particularly inflamed him by hammering the floor with his cane. Richard knew there would be no reprieve. He waited for McAllister to finish.

"Long live the spirit of the independent, objective, critical thinker, without which, our democracy cannot exist.
> (Signed) Richard Chase, M.D.
> Third International Symposium, Doctors Against War
> June 2004"

McAllister thrust the paper toward Richard.

"Sound familiar?"

Richard stood up and walked toward McAllister. "Yes, I wrote it, and I read it aloud to a group of people. Yes, I walked in marches. Yes, I gave money."

"Sit down."

"I will *not* sit down, sir. You need to listen to what—"

"Sit down!"

The two men glared at each other, their angry faces nearly touching. Richard lowered himself onto the oak chair behind him.

"Now, I understand," McAllister began, in an uncharacteristically soft tone, "that we Americans all have a God-given right to our personal opinions about politics and religion and the like. So, my young man, as much as it pains me, I'm not angry with you because you don't happen to share my vision for this grand country. You don't have to agree with me to be my friend." The softness in his face suddenly disappeared. "But, there is one thing that I will absolutely not tolerate, and that is personal insult."

"Personal insult? Mr. McAllister, I simply—"

"Criticizing President Bush is one thing, but when you criticize our troops, these brave men and women, risking their lives—this is intolerable! What's more, you have the gall to blame their families. And the church—the very heart and soul of our society, the foundation of our country. How can you say or even think these things and still call yourself a proud American?"

Richard shook his head. "Mr. McAllister, I am *not*—"

"And if that weren't enough, you couldn't even seem to keep your mouth shut at work."

Richard frowned. "What?"

McAllister shook his cane toward Richard.

"Seems you couldn't stop telling nurses, other doctors, even patients what you think, whether they wanted to hear it or not—bashing the president, holding everybody involved responsible, especially the troops. Spouting off about how Bush and his cronies are evil, terrorists even, and all the troops are mindless idiots."

Richard stood up. "Excuse me? I've never in my life—"

"Oh no? That's not what I heard. Word has it you brought some nurse to tears, one who had a son in Iraq when we first went in, after you said that no decent parent would allow their child to be a part of this mission. Do you deny this?"

Richard's eyes widened. Anger and incredulity filled him.

"Yes! I certainly do deny it, absolutely, positively deny it."

"Deny, deny, deny. That's all you can do, is it?"

McAllister threw a shaky hand back into his pocket and yanked out the speech he had read.

"But you can't deny this, can you?" He shook his fist in the air. "How can you deny it there when you already said it here? By God, I may be an old man with my best fighting days far behind me, but I promise you, I am no fool, and you will not treat me like one. Have you already forgotten 9/11? Three thousand innocent Americans incinerated."

"I never in my life said those things to any of those people. Never. Who fed you those absurd lies?"

McAllister replaced the speech in his pocket and jabbed at the tiny space between them with his cane.

"Dictators, religious fanatics. People have no control, no freedom. A land without democracy, without freedom, is a breeding ground for terrorism. Am I not right?"

"Yes, but will you listen to me?"

"Best way to fight terrorism? Squash dictatorships. Give people democracy. Destroy the governments that support terrorism. That's what this great, freedom-loving country is trying to do. Democracy, freedom, and, I also don't mind saying, some good, old-fashioned Christian values. Surely you agree that the people of the Middle East deserve democracy and freedom, don't you?"

"Yes, everybody on the planet deserves to live in a democracy, but it's not that simple."

"Don't patronize me, young man. Where would we be if we hadn't answered FDR's call after Pearl Harbor? You think we knew everything that was happening on the other side of the world? Hell, no! We were attacked, and we responded, like my grandson responded."

Richard paused. "Your grandson?"

"Andrew James McAllister, named after his only living grandfather. Two tours of duty in Iraq, I'm proud to say."

With the wave of his cane, McAllister pointed to a pair of chairs next to a large window. The two men sat with less than a foot between their knees—Richard on the edge of his seat, McAllister hunched forward, hands on his knees, slowly shaking his head.

"Never forget that day. Came over here to talk to me before enlisting. He was full of questions. We talked for hours. I could see that fire in his eye. I knew he wanted to go. He just wanted my support, my blessing. Well, I gave him that blessing. That bright, handsome young man, who I love as much as anybody in the entire world. I gave him my blessing."

Richard shook his head.

"Sir, I didn't—"

"Oh, yes you did, my young man. It's all there in that speech of yours, all fancied up with twenty-dollar words, but still plain as day. What do you think we are? Mindless sheep? Warmongers? Is that what you think this family is? Is that what Andy is? Is that what I am, Dr. Chase?"

"Your grandson. Is he okay?"

McAllister glared at Richard for a moment, and then turned his head away and sighed. "He got home in one piece, if that's what you're asking. Yes, he's okay, thank God."

Had Richard unwittingly touched on the only common ground they shared over this catastrophe, the value of a human life? He looked directly into the old man's eyes. "Mr. McAllister, I'm not going to torture you with my political views. You already know how I feel. But I must say this: On my word of honor as a man and physician, I never, ever made those hateful comments to those people. Whoever told you that is a malicious liar. I deeply apologize for any pain my views have caused you and your loved ones. I intended no harm. I deeply admire your military record and the bravery of your grandson. I am not a pacifist. I'm as patriotic as the next American and want to fight terrorism. I just disagree with what we did, that's all." He paused, lowered his voice, and said with resolve, "I can't and won't change the way I feel, no matter what."

Richard waited. He glanced at the blueprints resting on the chair, then back to McAllister, peering into his eyes. McAllister tilted his head slightly, squinted, and rubbed his chin. A moment later, he pushed himself out of his chair and strolled across the room to a window overlooking a large garden. He waved Richard over with his cane.

"Come over here. I want to show you something."

Richard approached the window and stood next to McAllister. A grove of mature oak trees bordering a large grass pasture filled their view. McAllister tapped the glass with a crooked finger and smiled.

"Pretty nice, huh?"

Richard studied the old man's wrinkled, smiling face, looking for any signs that the impasse was over. McAllister had always been honest and transparent with his feelings. Evidently, a few minutes of vitriolic condemnation was all he had needed. Richard had stuck to his guns and survived. He thought of the blueprints resting on the chair behind him and broke into a warm smile.

"Yes indeed. Very nice view."

McAllister slapped Richard on the back and laughed. "I knew we'd agree on something."

Richard broke away to retrieve the blueprints, echoing the laugh. "You'd be surprised. We probably agree about more than you think."

"Tell you what," McAllister said. He cleared his throat. "I'd like to make you an offer, a very generous offer, I might add. I wouldn't even consider it if, well, I didn't like you so damned much. You can keep those misguided ideas of yours, but I don't want to catch you shooting off your mouth about it. If the topic ever comes up again, you must avoid it or decline comment in private or public. No WPAW, no speaking engagements, no marching. In return, all will be forgiven. I will welcome you into our personal and business families and never again speak about this."

Richard's mouth fell open. "Excuse me?"

"You heard me. I'm giving you the chance to start fresh."

The blueprints, resting in Richard's arms like a baby, slipped from his fingers, falling to the floor. "What are you saying?"

"Go home and think it over. It's a generous offer."

"What if I refuse?"

McAllister slammed his cane onto the windowsill, rattling the glass. "Then you're a damned fool! By Jesus, how could you possibly walk away from this chance of a lifetime? Isn't that what you called it yourself?"

Richard spoke in a raspy whisper. "You'd revoke our agreement?"

"It doesn't have to be that way, for God's sake. Just give me your word, and we'll forget we ever had this unpleasant business."

Richard, silent and motionless, stared through McAllister, trying to comprehend. His eyes fell to the blueprints, partially unraveled on the floor between them. He picked up his beloved scroll and ran his fingers slowly over the grainy paper. He lifted his head to face McAllister. Behind and above the old man's face, the large, tattered flag caught his eye. He smiled and handed McAllister the blueprints.

"Excellent, my boy! I knew you'd—"

"No!" Richard shook his head slowly. His fear and anger vanished. "You can keep them. They're no good to me anymore."

McAllister pulled back his hand as if he'd just been bitten, sending both his cane and the blueprints flying to the floor.

"What? What did you just say?"

With a quiet defiance, Richard softly gave the only answer he could. "I'm sorry. I can't do that. I can't give you that promise."

McAllister fell back several steps. "Are you out of your mind? Do you realize what you're throwing away? Why? For what?"

"You want to know why?" Richard picked up the cane and aimed it at the flag above the double doors. "That's why. You're not the only patriot in this room."

McAllister stiffened. "Who the hell do you think you are?"

Richard handed McAllister his cane and smiled. "I do believe you dropped this."

McAllister snatched the cane and delivered a savage blow to the floor between them.

"You're going to regret this, young man. I'm warning you!"

"Good day, sir."

Richard turned and briskly headed for the double doors. Before leaving, he stopped, took one final glimpse at the flag, and turned toward McAllister.

"If only you could understand—we really all want the same thing."

Richard strode past three astonished house servants conspicuously huddled in the entryway, stepped out into the cool spring air, and sped down the driveway.

A scattering of dead leaves from last autumn flew up behind him.

Richard sped through the streets of Boston, soaked with sweat. The nightmarish blur of the past hour repeatedly flashed through his mind.

How can this be happening? I never said those things. Lies, all lies.

Who in God's name could have done this? Who could have stooped to such a ghastly level of maliciousness? He flew down a narrow, one-way street lined with cars. Nothing mattered but to identify the scum who had done this. Anguish and grief suddenly had a new partner—obsession.

Who hated him? He immediately excluded McAllister. He would never have fabricated those lies. Someone must have—

A muffled ring came from his jacket in the back seat. He awkwardly retrieved the phone and checked the number—*home*.

"Hello."

"Richard? Is everything okay, sweetheart?"

"I'm coming home."

"Jesus, you sound awful. Are you okay?"

He snapped the phone shut and threw it onto the passenger seat.

Thirty minutes later, he roared in through his front door.

Leslie met him in the hallway, nearly bumping into him. "Richard, what's wrong? What happened?"

He opened his mouth to speak, but shook his head. She grasped his arm. He pulled away.

"Honey, what happened?"

"McAllister found out about my anti-war activities."

"What? What in the world are you talking about?"

"Remember when I marched and wrote that letter about the Iraq war? Well he found out about it. But that's not the worst part. He also accused me of acting like some crazed lunatic, shooting off my mouth to everyone at the hospital, ramming my views down everyone's throat."

"Shooting off your mouth? Where the hell did he get that?"

"I have no idea. He wouldn't tell me. Some malicious bastard must have fed him all this shit. He knew everything— my marching, WPAW affiliation, donations I made. He even had a copy of part of a speech I gave last year and read it to me. Turns out he is a passionate supporter of the Iraqi invasion. Served in World War II. Has a grandson who went to Baghdad, for Christ's sake. Told me I've personally insulted him with my views. Said if I didn't end all my activities and keep my mouth shut, he'd pull the offer, the whole damned thing."

"Keep your mouth shut? So what did you say?"

Richard glared at her. "What do you think I said?"

Leslie smiled. "Good for you. I hope you told him to kiss your ass."

Richard smacked the banister with his hand. "I just can't imagine who would have done this to me, after all this time."

"Oh, come on. McAllister has a large, powerful family and lots of friends in high places. Probably someone knew about your activities and brought them to his attention."

"Yeah, okay, but why lie about it? You should have heard him, for Christ's sake. Made me sound like some nut case."

"Maybe he felt he needed a better reason to pull out of the agreement. You know, to save face."

"Then why would he give me the option of letting it all slide if I keep my mouth shut and be a good boy? It doesn't make any sense. Anyway, I doubt he thinks he needs an excuse for anything."

"Fuck him. We'll do it without him."

Richard threw up his hands. "No, Leslie, we can't. Not after the money we . . . *I* lost. And none of the other GI guys I would care to work with want to invest that kind of money."

Leslie ran her hands through her mass of curls. "I don't know, Richard."

"Jesus, Leslie, I just saw my dream go down the drain for something I didn't say! Do you understand that?"

Leslie hugged and kissed him. "Yes, my love. I do. I just wish . . . I don't know. It's not the only dream worth having, that's all."

"You're right, Les. It's not, but that doesn't mean I should just roll over and play dead." He turned toward the office, and then spun back to her. "Something stinks to high heaven here. You know it and I know it. Well I promise you, as I stand here now, I'm going to get to the bottom of this."

He marched into his office and slammed the door behind him.

The next morning, Richard reluctantly lifted his weary body out of bed. He stumbled into the shower, turned on the water, and got out without touching the soap. He stared at his cereal in the bowl, unable to eat. After putting on the same clothes he had worn on Friday, he fell behind the wheel of his car and dragged himself to the office.

As he pulled into his parking spot, Richard realized he had a procedure scheduled thirty minutes earlier at Trinity Hospital on the other side of town. Ordinarily, such a gaffe would have infuriated him. But this morning, he shrugged, turned around, and went to Trinity.

Three hours later in his office, while pretending to listen to a patient with abdominal pain, Richard considered Leslie's comment—that the whole thing was probably a McAllister concoction. Improbable as it seemed, wasn't that the simplest diagnosis? Why involve others if you didn't have to? He tried to prepare himself for this grim reality. He had a right to be angry. But how could he avenge himself on an old man, surely close to the end of his life, even if he had manufactured those lies?

Yet to let this go unpunished . . .

But what could he do?

At four o'clock, Richard found himself at his desk, staring

at a half-empty cup of black coffee. Where had the day gone? He had sleepwalked through procedures in the early morning, a lecture to medical students, a tasteless lunch, rounds, and finally, a few private patients in his office.

He looked out the dirty window between the slightly angled wooden blinds into a small grove of woods at the back of his office. The small wooded area, about a quarter acre filled with maple and oak, was part of the property on which his ten-year-old, two-story office rested. How beautiful this little wooded area was.

The door slowly opened. John Sharkey, one of the two young gastroenterologists Richard had hired to help grow his practice, stood before him.

"Hey, Richard, I hope you don't mind my asking, but is everything okay? You look like you've been run over by a train."

"Actually, I am feeling a little under the weather. But I'm okay."

"You sure?" Sharkey shifted his lanky frame in the doorway.

Leave it to Sharkey to see right through him. He considered holding his ground, but maybe he should at least tell his two associates about the change of plans.

"John, is Terry around?"

"Yeah, I think he's out front finishing up some dictations."

"Would you mind getting him? I've got a little news to tell you guys."

Sharkey's face turned ashen.

Richard forced a reassuring smile. "Hey, it's not as bad as that. Go on, go get him."

A minute later, Sharkey and Terry Gilham, a thirty-two-year-old South African, came into Richard's office. Richard pulled his tired eyes away from his trees. Gilham, the quieter of the two young men, sat on the edge of his chair. Sharkey sat forward, rubbing his hands.

Richard sighed deeply and looked down at his desk.

"I wasn't going to say anything, but John told me I looked like shit, so I guess I may as well tell you both why. McAllister has withdrawn his offer to fund our new endoscopy center. I can't do it myself, so the project is off."

Gilham jumped up. "Why'd he do that?"

Richard felt his face flush. He kept his head down and tapped his fingers on the desk.

"I don't know. He didn't say."

Richard hoped the lie wasn't conspicuous. He lifted his head and smiled stoically. "Easy come, easy go, boys. That's life."

Gilham shrugged. "Hey, we're just glad you're okay, that's all."

Richard cleared his throat. "Thank you, guys. I was going to tell you eventually, but I'm glad I told you now."

Sharkey and Gilham rose, each muttering a clichéd condolence, and disappeared.

Richard turned to the window. He made a halfhearted effort to get up, but found himself barely able to move. Perhaps he would just sit here.

A light knock came at the door. Richard found Sharkey again standing before him.

"Boss, could I speak to you for a minute?"

Richard pointed to the chair.

"I'm not sure how to say this, but I think I may know why McAllister cancelled his offer."

Richard straightened in his chair. "What?"

"He was at the medical staff meeting Friday night to pick up some award. After the meeting, I just happened to overhear a conversation between him and Jack Lundh."

"Lundh?"

"I started walking over to them, but then McAllister blurted something out in anger. I didn't hear what he said—they sort of had their backs to me—but I could tell he was pissed, so I froze in my tracks. Next thing I knew, McAllister started talking about the war against terrorism. I was about to get the hell out of there, but then Jack said something about unpatriotic doctors. I didn't catch it exactly. I took out my cell phone and pretended to make a call. McAllister asked who they were. Lundh hesitated and then started talking about marching and money and speeches."

Richard pounded his fist onto the desk, rattling his coffee cup and radio.

"Jesus! What did he say? What *exactly* did the son of a bitch say?"

Sharkey stood up and shook his head.

"I don't know exactly. I couldn't hear every word. Something about upsetting a whole bunch of people in the hospital—staff, nurses, even patients—telling them about how the troops shouldn't have been there. Stuff like that. You should've seen McAllister; he looked incensed. Without being asked again, Jack *offered* to give the name of this really bad guy, the worst of the bunch, but *only* if McAllister promised to keep it to himself. That's when I heard your name."

Richard gasped.

"I can't believe this. It's impossible!"

"I heard McAllister say something like 'show me' or something like that. Then I saw Lundh scribbling on a pad. Last thing I heard before my cell actually went off was something about Lundh coming over Tuesday to see a scrapbook. Old war mementos, I think."

"What? McAllister invited him over? Tomorrow night?"

"That's what it sounded like."

"Anything else?"

"No. The second my cell went off, I got the hell out of there."

"They see you?"

"No way. They were too wrapped up in each other."

Richard turned toward the window and viciously smacked the wall with an open hand.

"I can't believe it. I can't *fucking* believe it."

"Believe me, Richard, I'm as shocked as you are about this. I don't know what to tell you. Are you going to be okay? I mean, if you want to talk . . ."

Richard turned toward Sharkey. "No. I'll be fine. I think I'll sit here alone a few minutes."

Once Sharkey left, Richard looked out the window, but instead of seeing his little grove of trees swaying in the light breeze, his anguished mind could only see that horrible conversation taking place. The frightfully crisp image of Lundh's malicious declarations burned him like acid. He swung around, knocking over his paper shredder, and pounded both fists onto his desk. He snatched a porcelain figurine of a smiling, old country doctor given to him years ago by a grateful patient, raised it above his head to smash into smithereens against the door. Then he froze. He gently replaced the precious item onto his desk.

Oh my God. What's happening to me?

Richard left the office and headed home. Fifteen minutes later, he burst through his front door and slammed it behind him. Leslie met him in the hallway, next to the grandfather clock. He couldn't tell her fast enough.

"Jack Lundh!"

She frowned. "What?"

"Remember Jack? You met him at the staff party last year. General surgeon. I wouldn't let him operate on our dog. I told you somebody was behind all this. Son of a bitch!"

"Richard, calm down! What the hell are you talking about?"

"John Sharkey overheard the whole damned thing."

When Richard had finished, Leslie lowered her head and sighed.

"I don't know, Richard. It all sounds so crazy."

"It all fits. Lundh knows I'm a member of the WPAW. I never went around soliciting members, but it's pretty well common knowledge. The rest of the stuff is on the Internet."

Richard ran his hands through his hair and grimaced.

"Remember that photograph of Godfrey and me marching in Providence in 2003? The rest, the son of a bitch made up, just to make sure McAllister would be disgusted enough to drop me like a hot potato."

Leslie grasped Richard's hand. "Look, sweetheart, I know how passionate you can be about your feelings. Are you sure you didn't get yourself into, well, discussions with anyone recently?"

Richard pulled away. "Discussions? You've got to be kidding me. Have you ever seen me talking about this stuff at parties unless someone asked me—even after a few drinks?

No! I have *never* pushed this on anybody! You know how I feel about that."

"Yeah, I know, but I just don't get it. Why would this surgeon go to the trouble of doing all this, especially lying, after all this time? That's pretty nasty. Does he have a reason to hate you?"

"A good reason?" Richard smirked. "No. But something did come up between us."

He paced briskly from the kitchen to the front door, and then turned to Leslie.

"You know how I'm on the Quality Assurance Committee at the hospital. Well, about a year ago, it came to our attention that his complication rate and injuries during gallbladder removals might have been unacceptably high. After looking at his cases over the last two years, we determined it was *very* high. The son of a bitch is a butcher. Everybody hemmed and hawed, but nobody wanted to do anything other than notify him of our findings. I was the only one who spoke out, insisting he go to a refresher course on the procedure."

Leslie smiled a bittersweet smile. "I should have known."

"People objected, saying it was unreasonable. 'What about the patients?' I asked. Anyway, after considerable deliberation, my recommendations were finally carried out, much to Lundh's dismay. His next twenty cases were monitored. And guess what? His numbers got better. But, was he pissed."

"Is that it? That doesn't sound like enough for him to go after you."

"There was one other thing. Remember that morning I went in to see McAllister when he was sick? Well, Lundh was called in to do a gallbladder removal. The patient's oldest son pulled me aside and asked me, point blank, was I okay with Lundh as the general surgeon."

"And you said no."

"Not exactly. I just frowned and shook my head."

"Terrific."

"What the hell did you want me to say? He's the greatest surgeon on earth? I'm sorry, but if I've accepted the responsibility of trying to save this guy, I'm not going to mislead the family about the quality of the surgeon. Anyway, the son asked me, in confidence, which surgeon I would pick if the patient were my father. So I gave him a name, two names actually. We ended up going with Chris."

"What did Lundh say about this little switcheroo?"

"He confronted me in the lounge. He all but accused me of having him kicked off the case. Said he heard it from a nurse. I was pissed and told him that the family simply chose another surgeon. Actually, I told him he was lucky to have gotten out of it, but he didn't buy it, the bastard."

"Look, I agree. It sounds like you got royally screwed, but there's no point getting yourself worked up into a frenzy. You look like you're ready to bust. I know it's not going to be easy, but mark my words, as tough as it may sound, the best thing to do is just put it behind you."

"Put it behind me? The son of a bitch slanders me, and I'm going to let it go?"

"What the hell are you going to do, sue him?"

"You're damned right I'm going to sue him, for all he's worth, the bastard!"

"Oh come on, Richard. Based on what? An employee eavesdropping on a private conversation? You think for one second McAllister's going to admit to that conversation? Are you nuts? All you'll achieve is to further deplete what savings we have."

Richard paced up and down the hall, shaking his head.

"So you expect me to just walk away and forget it ever happened? Leslie, I've been raped, for Christ's sake!"

Leslie rushed toward him. "You have *not* been raped! Unjustly treated, screwed over, but not raped. You want to know what rape is? Ask my sister. You want me to get her on the line?"

Richard lowered his head. "I'm sorry."

"I understand it's a bitter pill to swallow, but you really don't have a lot of options. Why don't you write him a scathing letter? Even tell him you plan to proceed with legal action. Who knows what'll come of that? At the very least, you'll give him something to worry about."

Richard lifted his head and looked into her eyes. "It's not right, Leslie. It's just not right."

"I know, sweetheart. Please listen to me. Write the letter. Go on into your office and write it now, while you're still boiling. Send it off in the morning and be done with it. Do you hear me?"

Richard looked at her for a moment, and then nodded. "I guess you're right."

Leslie smiled. "Go on, get writing. I'm going to bed. Goodnight, dear. I love you."

She kissed him and went upstairs.

A moment later, Richard found himself in his office, staring at the blank screen. He typed the date and attempted a salutation.

Dear . . .

He smacked the delete button and fell back into his chair. He remembered he had forgotten to tell Leslie about Lundh being invited to McAllister's estate tomorrow evening. He leapt up the steps two at a time, but stopped at the second-floor landing. He sat on the top step, hung his head, and sighed. What difference was it going to make?

Leslie was such a mystery—emotional, passionate, fiery temper—the quintessential artistic temperament. Yet, for all that, here she was, the calm, rational one. And here he was, the doctor, the master of calm and rationality in the operating room, now feeling brutalized and mad as hell. Where was her fiery temper now, when he so desperately needed her? Would she be as "rational" if someone had stolen her paintings or unfairly criticized her work?

Richard pulled himself to his feet and froze. *Wait just one minute.* He did have another option here, didn't he?

He flew down the stairs and into his office. Lundh was having his little rendezvous with his new best friend McAllister tomorrow night. What a fabulous opportunity to "set the record straight" with both of them. Richard would discreetly tail Lundh to McAllister's estate, surprise Lundh as they reached the gates, and suggest the two of them go on in and have a friendly chat with the Grand Poobah.

But would it work? What if Lundh refused to listen? What if McAllister didn't let them in?

Richard could visualize the scene. He could pull ahead of Lundh and block his access to the gates without drawing attention from inside. Lundh would have no choice but to cooperate. But could that be considered harassment? With

Richard's luck, Lundh would have the cops on speed dial. Richard pictured himself—angry and humiliated—escorted home by the city's finest. Suddenly, the brilliant idea wasn't looking as attractive.

What if, what if. Where was that going to get him? Sure, he may hit a bump or two in the road. But even if it did entail some risk, this was a golden opportunity for some real vindication. He wouldn't block the gates; that was too big a risk. Instead, he would confront his nemesis right there and then.

For the first time since that dreadful call last Sunday morning, Richard began to feel lightness, even exhilaration, as if his suffocating burden had been made just a touch less heavy. He might have been wounded terribly; but by God, he wasn't about to roll over and die.

The following evening, Dr. Jack Lundh hopped into his car, inserted his favorite CD, and gave himself a congratulatory smile in the rearview mirror. He checked his watch—seven— more than enough time to make his eight o'clock date with the ultra-powerful J.P. McAllister for a nostalgic visit back to World War II.

Jack wasn't particularly interested in watching McAllister waltz down memory lane, but so what? All that counted was the invitation. McAllister's anger and vehement condemnation of Richard Chase after the medical staff meeting had been gratifying enough, but the invitation was an unexpected plus. Not only might he succeed in delivering a long-overdue punch in the mouth to Chase, but if Jack played his cards right, he might gain the favor of one of the richest families in the country.

What if he was sucking up? When opportunity knocks, bust down the door.

Jack pulled out of his gated subdivision in Bayport, an upscale neighborhood of about three-hundred homes south of Boston. Forty-seven minute drive time, according to his navigational system. He wouldn't want to lose his way; he might have to call Chase for directions. He burst out laughing.

As he cruised along Beacon Street, Jack thought about

the WPAW newsletter, with the priceless photo of Dr. Richard Chase marching. He smiled thinking about Chase's "sermon from the mount." If that hadn't fed the old man's indignation, nothing would. He wondered if McAllister would say anything about them. But only one question really mattered. Had he done enough to bury the center?

Jack knew it was best to keep quiet. He didn't want to bring into question the sincerity and noble intent of his comments. He would be the perfect gentleman. If offered, he would restrict himself to one drink. He would be especially careful not to lead or force a conversation. If McAllister felt an inclination to discuss Chase or the ambulatory center, that would be so much the better. Never, ever give the old man any reason to be suspicious. Jack had done his job. He would keep his mouth shut and hope for the best.

A quick glance at the gas gauge showed it was near empty. As he filled the tank of his new, navy Mercedes coupe, Jack felt a pang of doubt tinged with guilt. Had Chase's indiscretions really been nasty enough to warrant retaliation? The pump flew past twenty-five dollars. His face burned thinking about the humiliation he had suffered in front of his peers, and having such an important patient stolen from right under his nose.

Yes, more than nasty enough.

As he pumped gas, Jack relived the anger he had felt when he heard that Chase had been offered a business partnership with McAllister. He had first become suspicious when he saw the article announcing the McAllister family's plans to build an ambulatory medical facility in Cambridge, "details to be forthcoming." He knew that Chase owned commercial property in Cambridge on which he planned someday to build an endoscopy center. After a few well-placed calls, Jack's suspicions were confirmed. Chase had sold the land to a corporation called Freedom Medical, which happened to be owned by none other than McAllister and Chase.

Jack slammed the nozzle into its holder. Had he done the right thing? He smiled.

You're damned right!

He slid behind the wheel and shook his fist in triumph. Yes sir, things were definitely looking up, starting tonight. He couldn't wait to see his good friend, Mr. McAllister.

—⁂—

As the Mercedes pulled out, a white SUV emerged from its hiding spot at the adjacent fast-food restaurant, bypassed the pump area, and pulled onto the busy two-lane street.

Richard's jaw tightened as he clenched the SUV's steering wheel. He wove in and out of the traffic. With a burst of acceleration, he managed to position himself one vehicle removed from Lundh. An angry horn blasted from behind. Richard threw up his hand in apology.

Damn, this tailing thing isn't as easy as I thought.

He glanced at the empty front passenger's seat. How he wished Leslie were next to him, right now, supporting him, proud of him, eager to help defend his good name.

The traffic slowed to a crawl. Cars were packed tight without any openings for as far as Richard could see. In the distance, he thought he could see big yellow arrows pushing traffic right.

Nothing he could do now except crawl along with the rest of them. The Mercedes was now three cars ahead of him.

Please, don't let him slip away from me.

Moments later, Richard watched helplessly as the Mercedes turned right onto a small residential street and disappeared. He tried to cut over from the left lane to chase the slippery bastard, but a wall of cars blocked his way. He pounded the wheel. He scanned the street map on his navigational system.

Maybe I can take another way and catch up with him.

The cars in front of him stopped. His heart sank. Without even trying, that miserable bastard had managed to shake him off.

A few minutes later, he finally wriggled past the construction and stomped on the gas. He would have preferred to catch Lundh before the visit, but no matter. Richard would go to McAllister's estate, park outside the gates, and wait. By the time the night was out, he would have that little weasel's balls in a vice.

Ten minutes later, Richard arrived at McAllister's estate. The single-lane country road running along the front of the property had a generous dirt and gravel shoulder on both sides. He spotted a suitable location just off the side of the road in front of a vacant property opposite McAllister's, well away from any gate surveillance. He'd wait all night if necessary.

Richard opened his window a crack, partially reclined his seat, and positioned his head to keep an eye on a corner of the gate. He checked his watch: eight fifteen. As soon as he saw the nose of the Mercedes at the gates, he would cut across the street and rush along the shoulder to block Lundh's exit onto the road.

The minutes ticked by slowly without a stir from anything other than the gentle rustle of the leaves and the passing of an occasional vehicle. Dim lights from black lampposts decorating the top of the stone wall now bathed the street.

Nine fifteen came and went.

What the hell are they doing in there?

A police cruiser pulled up behind him. Startled, Richard straightened the back of his seat and took out his cell phone. The policeman, a tall, thin man in his early fifties, slowly approached Richard's SUV.

"Good evening, sir. Can I ask you what brings you here tonight?"

"Good evening, Officer. I just pulled over to answer a call about a sick patient at the hospital. I'm Dr. Chase."

A glimmer of recognition flashed across the officer's face. "Dr. Chase? The GI doctor?"

Richard forced a smile. "Yes, yes, that's me."

"Well I'll be darned. I thought I recognized you. You did my wife, Carmella Hurt." He wiggled his index finger with a sheepish smile. "You know, the colon scope, about six months ago. Our family doc said you were the best."

Richard felt his muscles relax. "Oh, yes, I remember now. How is Carmella?"

"Just fine, Doc. Thank you. Hey, sorry for interrupting your call. People across the street called. Picked you up on their surveillance a few minutes ago and wondered what you were doing here. You know these rich types. They get nervous about this kind of thing."

Out of the corner of his eye, Richard saw the gates starting to open. The nose of the blue Mercedes crept forward. A moment later, the car was gone. Richard flashed a smile to conceal his boiling insides. "I'm sorry to have taken up your time, Officer. I should be getting to the hospital."

"Oh, sure, Doc. Have a great night."

Richard pounced on the power window control and cursed under his breath. Damn his rotten luck.

Controlling an urge to peel off the shoulder, Richard pulled onto the road, passed the front of the property without looking at the gate, and headed down the long country road. If he hurried, could he possibly catch up with Lundh before he passed through the gates of his development? No, not a chance . . .

The thought of that contemptuous scumbag going home to his wife made him sick. How she could sleep with that crock of shit was anybody's guess. She sure as hell wouldn't touch him if she knew about his little piece of ass on the side. For all he knew, that slimy bastard was probably running off to see her now, to celebrate his victory. Richard imagined him driving away, smiling broadly after a satisfying night of sucking up to McAllister. He wished he could wipe that smile off his face. If only he could somehow—

Richard caught his breath. He pulled onto the shoulder, skidding along the loose gravel, and came to an abrupt stop.

Lundh's dirty little secret.

Richard dismissed the crazy idea immediately. As much as he detested the bastard, he couldn't do anything like that. Anyway, how would it help him? His relationship with McAllister was shot, and his dream was down the toilet.

Richard thought again about writing a letter or confronting Lundh face-to-face, if need be. Perhaps Richard would set the record straight with McAllister, for what it was worth.

He took a deep breath, turned on the radio, and headed for home.

Richard arrived home just before eleven. With any luck, Leslie would be fast asleep. He parked the car in the driveway and entered through a side door. Things looked promising. The ground floor was dark and quiet, with only a dim light coming from the kitchen. The door to the basement was half open. He poked his head downstairs. No music or lights. She must be in bed.

As Richard crept up the spiral staircase, he heard muffled voices from Justin's bedroom to his right. To his left, dim light shone from under his own bedroom door.

The prospect, even if unlikely, of having to deceive Leslie sent an ache through his chest.

Richard knocked softly on his son's door.

"Come in."

Justin was lying on his bed, flipping through television channels.

"Hey, Son, how is it going?"

Justin's eyes remained fixed on the television. "Not bad."

"Listen, I was thinking—"

Justin's cell phone began to vibrate on his bed. He pounced on it. "Hey, man, what's up? Hang on a sec." He pulled the phone away from his ear. "Sorry, important call."

Richard smiled. "Sure. Goodnight, Son."

He shut the door, promising himself he'd ask Justin about playing golf this weekend.

Leslie lay in bed, flipping through a magazine, her mass of curls crowding her face.

"Hi, dear. I heard you had a great night out."

Richard caught his breath. "What do you mean?"

"Victor called. He told me you got called into the hospital before your game."

"Victor called?"

"Actually, he called to tell me you left your credit card at the tennis pro shop. He didn't want to bother you at the hospital. You can pick it up there tomorrow."

Richard yanked out his wallet and found the empty space. "Oh, damn."

"Why are you still taking night calls, anyway? Shouldn't your partners be doing that? For Christ's sake, Richard, you're the Chief of Gastroenterology. You lecture all over the world. You see patients from all over the country. I can't believe you still have to go in."

Richard stood rigid by his dresser, fingering the buttons of his shirt. Blood drained from his head.

"Richard, are you okay? What is it?"

"I didn't go to the hospital."

Leslie sat up. "What?"

"I followed Lundh to McAllister's house. I wanted to confront him before he went in, to set the record straight. But I lost him in traffic. I sat in front of the estate, waiting for him to leave, but a cop came along."

Leslie threw her magazine onto the floor. "A cop stopped you?"

"Keep it down, will you. Don't worry. He just happened to be the husband of one of my patients. I told him I pulled over to make a call. He was fine."

Leslie buried her hands in her hair. "Richard, what the hell do you think you're doing?"

"Jesus, Leslie, the son of a bitch slandered me!"

"I'm warning you, you're going to get yourself into a shitload of trouble. How could you do such a ridiculous thing? What in the hell did you expect to accomplish? Are you trying to get yourself arrested?"

Richard slammed a dresser drawer shut.

"You just don't get it, do you?"

Leslie sprang out of bed and faced him. "I'll tell you what I get. I see somebody who got a nasty, unfair slap in the face from life and who desperately feels the need to slap back. Fine. I understand that. Just do it right. Write your damned letter, one to each of them, with all the fury you can muster, and then be done with it! Now, please, honey, come to bed."

Richard slipped into his pajamas, climbed into bed, and gave her his usual kiss on the back of her neck.

"I'll pick up your card in the morning."

"Thanks, Les. I love you."

Leslie stared into the darkness of the room, unable to close her eyes, overcome with a vague, aching discontent. An hour later, Richard's barely audible snore finally signaled deep sleep. Against her will, she stole a glance at the letter on her end table and gritted her teeth. Richard wasn't the only Chase having a tough day. She quietly slid out of bed and dropped into the old, worn armchair by the window. With the help of dim light from a street lamp, her bloodshot eyes once again scanned this latest rejection from a major art gallery. She tore the paper into tiny pieces and watched as they flew through the air, silently landing on the carpet next to the bed.

She had thought she really had a chance this time. Why did she even bother? She suddenly felt a compulsion to run downstairs, gather up all her paintings, douse them with gasoline, and light a match. Instead, she smiled sadly. No, her passion owned her, come what may. Screw them all! She knew her work was worthy. Her art teachers, even the tough ones, had said as much—*remarkable talent.* Her last teacher had told her she had a rare gift for expressing the extremes of emotion in portrait work—sadness, pain, despair, anger, heartache, frustration, loneliness, and yes, even happiness. She thought of those many sad faces she was ready to destroy and suddenly felt comforted by them.

In the beginning, a pat on the back, by anyone, plus the joy the work brought was enough to sustain her. But not now. Now she wanted her work shown, not just locally, but by the people who counted in the art world. She wanted recognition and acclaim. She wanted respect.

Leslie glared at the fragments of paper scattered on the carpet and cursed.

Why does it have to be so difficult?

Of course, she knew why. In the art world, it wasn't just the quality of the work—it was who you knew. And while Leslie could rattle off the names of plenty of professional acquaintances in the art world, she didn't have the kind of connections that would earn her a showing. Never mind;

her day would come. She wouldn't quit. She'd succeed or die trying.

Leslie looked at Richard and sighed. They lived in the same house, had the occasional meal together at home, went out to dinner and the movies, and even had great sex. She loved her family, but, somehow, it wasn't enough.

She went to the bathroom and clicked on the light. The bleakness of her reality never seemed so apparent, so exposed. She swept back her hair and looked at herself in the mirror—a drawn, tired face, her long, dirty-blond curls hanging over her cheeks. With a sweep of her hand, she held back her hair and took a good, hard look. Her big hazel eyes and expressive mouth seemed to reveal a quiet sadness. She had always had a young-looking face with little-girl features. But tonight, her thirty-eight-year-old face looked old and tired.

She pushed her thoughts away as best she could, crawled back into bed, and closed her eyes, hoping sleep would come before daylight.

8

Richard flew through his Wednesday morning cases—six upper endoscopies, two colonoscopies, and three ERCPs—finishing just before noon. He glanced at his watch. Where had the morning gone? He had no doubt that to everyone around him, he was his usual, focused, efficient self. Little did they know that he couldn't take his troubled mind off McAllister, Leslie, and Lundh—especially that bastard Lundh.

Having just finished the work, Richard could barely remember the procedures. Had he gone into the duodenum on Mrs. Calixto? What about that lady with the chronic diarrhea? Had he traversed the ileocecal valve to look for Crohn's disease? Yes, of course he had. He must have. He shook off the questions and trudged back to his office.

Richard finished his last dictation shortly before one o'clock, when Sharkey appeared at his door and gave his boss a nervous smile.

A wave of heat shot through Richard. "What's wrong, John?"

Sharkey dropped his eyes to the carpet in front of the desk. "You didn't hear?"

"Hear what?"

Sharkey closed the door, sat down, and looked awkwardly

past Richard out the window. "I just saw Thompson in the lounge. He told me he was just asked to consider becoming a, uh . . ." He looked away.

"John, for Christ's sake, what is it?"

"A shareholder at McAllister's new endoscopy-surgery center."

Richard sat forward in his chair. "*What?* What did you just say?"

"Apparently, a bunch of other guys have also been approached."

"You're kidding me, right?"

Sharkey stood up and rubbed his hands. "I'm afraid that's not the worst."

Richard caught his breath and stiffened. Sharkey continued. "Lundh was appointed the medical director of the center."

The words hit Richard like a shotgun blast, thrusting him back into his chair. He opened his mouth, but nothing came out.

Sharkey lowered his head. "I can't believe it myself."

Richard sat motionless, his hands hung limp at his sides, his eyes unfocused. "Thank you, John," he said in a raspy whisper. "I think I need a few minutes alone."

"Of course. Call me if you want to talk, okay?"

Richard closed his eyes and raised his hands to his face, his hot breath filling his palms. Flashes of McAllister's words to him and Sharkey's replay of Lundh's remarks tightened his gut. The inferno from within cut him off from his senses, taking away the floor from under his feet, holding his body rigid as an iron bar.

Once alone, he sprang up and cried out a full-throated cry, as if he had just been shot in the back. With a single, massive, violent swipe of both arms, everything on the desk went flying. His computer monitor bounced off the wall and landed with a thud onto the thinly carpeted floor. On the walls, the ceiling, the floor, even in the trees, Richard could see only one grotesque face, squealing in victory. He fell back into his chair, looked at the mess on the floor, and wiped his sweat-soaked face.

Thank God they're still all off at lunch.

Richard slowly began to pick up the mess. He found his cell phone under his chair, fortunately still intact. He finished his cleanup and dashed home, barely aware of the road before him.

When he arrived home, Richard found Leslie and Justin in the kitchen. He forced a smile and headed up the stairs to his bedroom.

At dinner, he sat quietly, nodding pleasantly at the appropriate places in Leslie and Justin's conversation over job options for Justin that summer, all the while wanting to scream.

After Justin excused himself, Leslie reached across the table and caressed her husband's hand. "You're awfully quiet. Anything wrong, sweetheart?"

Richard took a deep breath. "McAllister's going ahead with his own outpatient center, on the other side of town. He appointed Jack Lundh the medical director."

Leslie's eyes widened. "What?" She shook her head. "I told you I had a bad feeling about that filthy-rich old man."

"Forget about McAllister. He's not to blame. That slimy bastard Lundh is behind all this."

"Wow." She squeezed his hand. "I'm so sorry, honey."

Richard stood up. "Well, enough is enough. I'm going down to that bastard's house—tonight—to pull him out of bed if I have to, and settle this once and for all."

Leslie gripped his arm. "Are you nuts? What's that going to accomplish? You're going to get yourself arrested."

"What the hell do you want me to do, Les, sit around and forget about it? To hell with that. I'm going to knock on his door and—"

"And what? Go barging into his kitchen, guns blazing, and make a scene? Look, I know how you feel. Believe me. I just think there's a better way."

"A better way? You mean the letter? Fine! I'll write the damned letter, I promise. I just need to settle this, man to man."

Leslie glared at Richard. He looked at her, stone-faced, defiant. She broke the momentary standoff with a loud, angry sigh. "All right, go if you need to. Go. Get it over with. Just don't do anything stupid."

Richard kissed her on the cheek. "Don't worry. I'll be back in a flash. This won't take long."

—∿∿—

Richard practiced his lines in the car. His stomach churned. A guard greeted him at the front gate.

"Can I help you, sir?"

"I'm visiting Dr. Jack Lundh. My name is Tynan. Just let him know Victor, one of his tennis buddies, would like to drop in."

The guard checked his clipboard and picked up a phone receiver.

"I'm sorry, sir. Nobody is answering."

"Nobody's answering? Maybe I can . . . never mind. Thank you."

Didn't the bastard play tennis every weekend? Hadn't Richard seen his name penciled in for a Saturday morning slot?

Yes, that's right; he plays with that radiologist, Gomez, on Saturday mornings. Perhaps he should run over to the club to check out the schedule.

The Black Diamond Tennis Club parking lot bustled with cars. Richard cautiously crept along the narrow rows, his progress slowed by numerous young families with their children darting between the closely packed vehicles. He looked for an empty space, all the while straining to see the blue Mercedes, but found neither. Finally, he spotted a family with three young children getting into their minivan. Richard squeezed into the vacated spot and sprinted to the front desk.

"Good evening, George."

A tall, elderly man with a full head of thick, white hair smiled. "Evening, Doc. How are you?"

"Fine. I'd like to have a look at the weekend sign-up sheet, if I may."

"Good luck, Doc. It looks pretty full already."

Richard scanned all three sheets—no Lundh.

"Hey, George, doesn't Jack Lundh play every weekend?"

"Every Saturday morning at ten. But I don't expect him to be around for the next eighteen days, though. He went to Hawaii with his wife and daughter on some kind of conference. He came in last night for a quick game. Nice guy, that Dr. Jack."

"Gone to Hawaii? Eighteen days?"

"Yep."

Minutes later, Richard rifled through a telephone book in the media room.

"Good evening. Dr. Lundh's answering service."

"Hello, I'm a patient of Dr. Lundh's. Ramon Campanero. I need to speak to the doctor. My back pain is getting worse."

"Sir, the doctor will be away until May 15. Dr. Lennon is taking—"

Richard slammed down the phone. He stood frozen, staring at his fist tightly clenching the receiver. A moment later, he dove into his pocket for his cell phone.

"Good evening, McAllister residence. May I help you?"

"Good evening. I'm Dr. Richard Chase. I would like to speak to Mr. McAllister, please."

"One moment, please."

Richard grimaced. His chest pounded. A flash of sweat came up on his brow. He threw his free hand against the wall for support and squeezed the phone.

"I'm sorry, but Mr. McAllister will not be taking your call tonight and requests that you not call him again. If necessary, any further communication should be through his attorney. Thank you, and have a good evening."

Richard staggered into a single-occupancy bathroom down the hall, slammed the door, and locked it behind him. The faux pleasantness of McAllister's butler made the rejection all the more humiliating. Richard turned his back to the door, slid down to the cold, tiled floor, and stared incomprehensibly at the dripping faucet.

Three tentative knocks at the door sent Richard scurrying to his feet. His cell phone fell out of his pocket onto the floor, the cover flying off. He muttered an obscenity under his breath, gathered up the pieces, and jammed them into his pocket.

"Ah, just a minute."

Richard flushed the toilet, briefly turned on the water at the sink, and then slowly opened the door. He brushed past a little boy and his mother, hurried out the front door, and fell in a heap behind the wheel of his car. He thought of Lundh sunning himself on the beaches of Hawaii and pounded the steering wheel.

The thought of waiting three weeks for that scumbag to return made his blood boil. All he could do now was wait. But for what? Everything he had tried up to now got him absolutely—

Richard caught his breath. He sat still, as if stunned. The idea, dismissed as unconscionable only several days earlier, now came roaring back.

Jack Lundh's dirty little secret.

What was her name? Linda? Or was it Angela? No matter. Chances are the news would hit his wife like a tsunami. He could just imagine the look on that pathetic bastard's face. Richard began to laugh, but stopped abruptly. A rush of heat shot into his face. He felt embarrassed, even ashamed. He buried his face in his hands.

Oh, God, am I going mad?

He then thought about what that reprehensible prick had done to him, to his honor, to his dream.

Shame and embarrassment vanished.

Blowing the whistle on an affair was one thing, but providing hardcore evidence was quite another. Richard strained to recall a former patient who had worked as a private investigator with special expertise in surveillance. Hadn't he claimed to be making money hand over fist chasing and bugging the legions of unfaithful husbands and wives in the city? Didn't that bastard's wife deserve to know what was going on? He smacked the center console with his fist.

He finally had a plan.

But where should he start? Where did one find such a person? He cringed at the notion of calling someone. He felt his nerve slipping away.

Calling someone first would be foolish. Before proceeding, he should educate himself a little about this surveillance stuff, shouldn't he? Let's see . . . he could pull it up online. Wait. What about the computer record? That couldn't be truly erased without destroying the hard drive. Damn, you can't move a muscle without being watched these days. Perhaps one of the major bookstores carried manuals on surveillance. He could stop by first thing in the morning. Yes, that was a good idea, wasn't it?

Richard wiped his face in his sleeve, took a few deep breaths, and sped home.

Richard awoke Saturday morning with thoughts of private investigators and surveillance swirling in his head. He glanced at Leslie and felt an impulse to wake her up and share his ideas, but resisted.

He jumped out of bed, showered, scribbled a note—*gone to bookstore, back by eleven, love*—and quietly slipped out. He buckled his seat belt and glanced up at the bedroom window. If only she were here sitting next to him.

An exhaustive search of the bookshelves yielded only a small manual on wiretapping telephone conversations. He inquired at the information desk about any other publications addressing surveillance. A pale, young woman wearing a gold necklace that read "Sara" squinted at her computer screen.

"Let's see. *The Professional's Comprehensive Guide to Audio and Video Surveillance.* It's not in stock, but I could have it here in a few days."

Richard hesitated. "Yeah, I think that will do. It's for my daughter, actually. She's doing a project on surveillance."

Sara smiled. "Your name?"

"Chase."

"Phone number?"

"Phone number? Yes, sure. I'll, uh, give you my cell."

"It'll be here by next weekend, probably. I'll call you when it's in."

Richard flung himself into his car, slammed the door shut, and smacked the steering wheel. What the hell was he doing giving his name and number like that? He should have just told her he would pick it up in a few days. How could he have been so careless?

Before heading home, he needed to purchase a phone with prepaid minutes to ensure confidentiality. He also wanted to stop by the library to run a search for private investigators in the Boston area. He would shorten his office hours next week, make some calls, and perhaps even pay a visit to a few private investigators.

He gave himself a cautiously optimistic look in the sun visor mirror, carefully pulled out of the busy parking lot, and drove off.

10

Richard glanced at his watch. How long was this guy going to keep him waiting? When he had seen his first of three private investigators several days earlier, his heart had been pounding with anticipation. Now, he held out little hope for getting any help. At this point, he just wanted to avoid the Friday afternoon traffic so he could get home in time for dinner with Leslie and Justin. He had forgotten to ask Justin about golfing this weekend. Sunday morning would be nice, if his son hadn't already made plans.

Richard sat in one of a pair of uncomfortable, upright wooden chairs facing each other in the tiny waiting room. Faded, dark-green-and-gold wallpaper curled at conspicuous seams along the walls. A long, narrow print of an orchid, including its extensive root system, hung on the door. A dusty, lopsided, fake plant filled a corner.

Four fifteen. He rubbed his eyes. Perhaps he should just cut his losses and leave. Why should this guy tell him anything different than all the others?

Yes, I spy on people, but I don't, or won't, or can't do what you're asking. That's illegal. Isn't everything they do bordering on illegal when you get down to it?

The wallpapered door opened. An early forties, overweight

man with thinning hair, enormous eyebrows, and a round face looked over his silver-rimmed spectacles at Richard and smiled.

"Who's next?"

Richard cleared his throat and stood up. "Ah, me, I think."

George J. DeBatista, private investigator, laughed, his fleshy neck rippling like waves in a pond.

"Mr. Addis, I presume?"

Richard nodded self-consciously at the mention of his fake name and extended his hand. "That's me."

"Sorry for the mess. They're renovating my place upstairs. I borrowed this hole-in-the-wall for a week from the owner. Thank God it's my last day here. Come on in."

DeBatista dropped into his chair behind his desk.

"Sorry about the delay. I had to tell a woman her husband wasn't the knight in shining armor she thought he was." He opened his notebook. "Now how can I help you?"

"A colleague of mine is having an affair. He brings the woman into his house when his wife is away. I want to record these secret rendezvous in his home, to catch them in bed and expose him to the man's wife."

DeBatista straightened in his chair and frowned. "Can I ask why?"

"He slandered me, resulting in the loss of a multimillion-dollar business opportunity."

"You've consulted an attorney?"

"No point. I wouldn't be able to prove a thing."

"Would it be possible to get your 'intelligence' outside the home?"

Richard sighed. "Yes, I suppose I could get pictures of

them meeting here and there, but that's not really going to help me much."

"It could still be damaging."

"Do I take it you're not able to consider my request?"

"Consider, yes. Carry out, no. A job like that is highly complicated, risky, and, most importantly, illegal." Richard nodded, stood up, and extended his hand. "I understand. Thank you for your time."

"Hang on," DeBatista said, ignoring Richard's gesture. "I could follow your bad boy around for a while. Maybe I can get lucky and catch them in an embrace or kissing. You never know. You'd be surprised what people do in their vehicles."

Richard shrugged.

"Mr. Addis, I'm not saying you couldn't find somebody to do the job, but I can tell you, something like that would cost you at least seventy-five to a hundred grand. The surveillance equipment alone would probably cost about ten grand."

Richard's eyes widened. "A hundred grand?"

"Give me a couple of weeks with them. No guarantees, but for a couple of hundred bucks, definitely less than a thousand, I might come up with something worthwhile. Cash upon delivery."

Richard drove home tired and depressed. He had agreed to have Batista do his thing, but he didn't feel optimistic for a big score. He found Leslie and Justin in the kitchen. He plugged his cell phone into its charger on the kitchen counter.

"Hi, guys."

"Hi, dear. Good timing. We just sat down."

Richard sat at the large, oval table opposite Justin.

"How was your day, Son?"

"Okay."

"Did Mom ask you about golf this Sunday?"

"Ah, yeah, she did. Sorry, I can't make it. Nate and I are going down to the auto show Sunday. I got the tickets last week."

"What about tomorrow?"

"I got soccer camp."

Leslie filled Justin's plate with chicken casserole.

"Hey, maybe you guys can hook up next weekend."

Richard nodded. "Sure. Good idea."

Justin remained silent. Ten minutes later, he excused himself.

Leslie gave Richard a smile of appreciation. "Maybe next weekend."

After clearing the dishes, Richard dragged himself into the shower. He twisted the showerhead from gentle to turbo-massage. As the jets of hot water pelted him, he thought about how foolish he had felt sneaking around and using a false name, as if he were committing some kind of crime. The thought of DeBatista following Lundh didn't give him much consolation. The bastard was too smart to be seen doing anything in broad daylight, at least not the things Richard wanted to catch him doing. He watched the soapy water swirl down the drain. Who knows, perhaps in a letter he could somehow find the perfect combination of savage condemnation and vague threat of legal action or retaliation to scare the pants off the bastard.

Richard twisted the water faucet off and stepped out. He was surprised to see Leslie, her brow furrowed, holding his cell phone out in front of her.

Richard froze, dripping wet. "What is it, Les? It isn't the hospital, is it? I'm not on call."

She yanked a towel off the rack next to her and threw it at him.

"It's the bookstore. It came up on your caller ID, so I answered it. Your *Comprehensive Manual of Surveillance* came in early. You can come and pick it up this evening."

Richard's insides tightened.

"What the hell do you need a book on surveillance for?"

He wrapped the towel around his waist and shrugged. "I couldn't figure out how that son of a bitch got all that information on me. I got it in my head that he may have been bugging my office or something."

Her eyes widened. "Bugging your office?"

Richard turned away toward the sink. Leslie squeezed herself between him and the countertop.

"You actually thought he was bugging your office?"

"Okay, so it was a crazy idea."

"You're damned right it's crazy! I knew something was up these last couple of days with this McAllister mess. You still haven't written that letter, have you? You're letting this thing eat you up like a cancer."

He looked down and sighed.

"Look sweetheart," she said, "I know you love your work and you're pissed about this mess, but you've got to stop letting your career take over your life, as if it were some kind of Holy Grail."

Richard pulled back. "Holy Grail? What about *your* Holy Grail?"

"What, my painting? At least I don't let it take over my

life. Look at your own seventeen-year-old son. He acts as if he doesn't even know you, or worse, doesn't *want* to know you, for Christ's sake."

That terrible day long ago flashed through Richard's mind. "Leave Justin out of this!"

"Okay, okay," she said softly. "Look, if it makes you feel any better, go get your damned book so you can figure out how you've been spied on. Just promise me you'll write that letter and get it out of your system."

"Yes, I promise. I plan to write it tonight."

Richard dried his hair, dressed quickly, and left to pick up the book before the store closed. He paid with cash, hurried out of the store, and escaped to his car, his heart pounding. He threw the package onto the back seat and delivered a savage blow to the dash just above the radio.

Damned sneaking around and lying . . .

A wave of nausea came over him. He started the car and turned up the music—a Jack Johnson tune—hoping the distraction would help, but the attempt was futile. He jabbed at a button, abruptly silencing the music, and drove home.

11

The following Tuesday, Richard drove to the tennis club for his usual evening match with Victor. His joints ached. Was he getting a sore throat? He couldn't be sure. He wondered if he had picked up some kind of virus from Mrs. Brunell, a patient with irritable bowel syndrome who had complained of similar symptoms in the office. Poor lady. She had been suffering ever since the death of her son a year earlier. He controlled her bowel problems easily enough, but he often wished he could help her with her sorrow. Perhaps instead of leaving her with his usual, sympathetic smile and another renewal for an antispasmodic, he would gently acknowledge her grief, and, well, just give her a hug.

What he wouldn't do for that kind of hug from Leslie.

Victor hadn't yet arrived. He checked his watch—thirty minutes before their match. He reached for his phone.

"Hey Vic. Do you mind if I take a rain check tonight? I feel like shit. I think I'm coming down with something."

Perhaps he should just sit at the bar and drink.

The lounge was packed and buzzing with the usual group of wealthy, suburban Bostonians. Richard surveyed the group sitting in their leather chairs surrounded by the mahogany furnishings and tasteful décor, no doubt discussing their successes of the day. He grimaced at the sight of them. What successes did he have to reflect on?

The only available empty seat was at the far end of the bar next to the wall, next to a rather unhealthy-looking ficus plant. Fortunately, the couple next to him was angled toward each other, absorbed in conversation. He gulped down his first Pinot Noir, barely tasting it. Usually, he would have sipped his favorite wine slowly and looked forward to his second glass, his normal limit. Not today. He drummed his fingers on the counter, held his head up with his other arm, and looked glumly at the dazzling array of spirits backstopping the bar. He pushed the empty glass away. Fiona, the Tuesday evening barmaid, approached him.

"Hey, Doc, can I get you a refill?"

Richard waved his hand in refusal. He pushed himself deeper behind the plant and became engrossed in a large, swirling knot in the wood on the bar next to his wine glass.

"Richard, is that you, hiding in the weeds?"

He spun around, nearly knocking over his wine glass. Dr. Cathy Wilcox stood before him.

"Cathy!"

"I'm sorry," she said. "I didn't mean to frighten you."

The couple next to Richard departed. He pulled one of the two vacated stools closer to him.

"No, not at all. It's good to see you. I didn't know you came here. Please, sit down. Would you like a drink?"

Cathy sat, crossed her long, slender legs, and swiveled towards him.

"Thank you. Water with a twist of lemon, please. I'm parched."

"Judging from the outfit, I'd say you've been working out."

"You don't miss a thing, do you, doctor? I thought I'd tighten up in a few places. I got the 'family' membership— for one."

Richard grinned. "Sounds like you're doing okay these days."

"You mean since I kicked out that cheating dog three months ago?" She laughed. "Things couldn't be better. During the day, Dr. Catherine J. Wilcox—family physician. When the whistle blows, Cathy, party of one, free and clear."

She raised her glass in a toast. "Down with all the deceitful bastards of the world!"

Richard raised his glass of water and attempted a smile. "I couldn't have said it better myself."

Cathy frowned. "Are you okay? Is something wrong?"

"Wrong? Yeah, you could say that."

Cathy glanced around the room and took a sip of water. "Do you want to talk about it?"

Richard took a slow, deliberate breath and nodded. "Yes, actually, I would like that."

A middle-aged man with remarkably hairy arms squeezed into the stool next to Cathy.

Richard stood up and anxiously scanned the room checking for familiar faces. "There's a little coffee place down the street called Shiba's."

Cathy nodded. "I know it. I'll see you there in . . . about fifteen minutes?"

Richard parked his car around the corner from the café and scanned the sidewalk. He recognized no one. At the doorway, he hesitated and peeked in. Nobody he knew. He found a seat in the back and sat facing a brick wall, drew in a long breath, and prepared himself for this unexpected catharsis.

After ordering coffee and dessert, they fumbled through some small talk about the deplorable state of Boston traffic, their respective medical practices—mostly the maddening increase in paperwork and ever-decreasing remuneration— and some benign hospital gossip. With the preliminaries over, Richard took a deep breath.

Cathy leaned toward him. "What is it, Richard? What's going on?"

"I don't even know where to begin."

The server interrupted. "Here you go. Two decafs. Here's the cream and sugar. You're going to love these pastries."

Richard sipped his coffee, buying a few moments to collect his thoughts. He placed the mug down and stared into the steaming black liquid.

"Remember I mentioned to you that I've always wanted to open my own endoscopy center?"

Richard leaned forward and told her everything, barely taking a breath. Cathy sipped her coffee and listened intently, her face gradually changing from quiet seriousness to concern, and then alarm. When Richard told her that Lundh had been made the CEO, her eyes widened in disbelief.

"You've got to be kidding me. Oh God, your blood must have been boiling. What did you do then?"

"I went straight to Lundh's house to confront the bastard. Turns out I just missed him. He pissed off to Hawaii with his wife. Can you believe that? Then I tried to get with McAllister, you know, to set things straight. He wouldn't see me. He wouldn't even talk to me. One of his hired guns told me that any further communication should be through his attorney."

"When is Lundh coming back?"

"About a week."

Cathy straightened in her chair and shook her head. "Wow, what a nightmare. I can't believe it. I mean, Jack Lundh?"

"I've played tennis with the guy for years. I even saw his patients, at least until that gallbladder fiasco."

Cathy chuckled. "Man, was he ever pissed."

"We actually did the son of a bitch a favor. And this is what I get for trying to do the right thing."

"That's the problem with being head of the committee."

"Listen, peer review is probably the only worthwhile meeting we have. I'll be damned if I'm going to let that scare me away. Somebody has to have the balls to stand up and do it. I didn't want to hurt the guy—personally or professionally. I don't expect him to put me on his Christmas list, but I don't deserve to be crucified."

"Have you thought of suing him?"

"Are you kidding? The hassle, the publicity, the cost. And for what? He'll deny saying anything slanderous. And don't expect McAllister to get himself mixed up in something like this. Even without the slander, he's already written me off. He'll just say it was a business decision. Leslie wants me to write Lundh a blistering, nasty letter, and threaten legal action. But what's that going to accomplish? Give me three minute's satisfaction?"

Cathy's shoulders straightened. Her fingers, busily playing with her spoon over a tiny fragment of éclair, froze.

"What does *she* think of this whole thing?"

"She understands, in a way, but she thinks I'm crazy for letting it make me so angry. The problem is, I can't control the way I feel. I've got such a ferocious anger."

Cathy resumed her game with the spoon. "So what are you going to do?"

Richard straightened in his chair. "Can I tell you something in confidence?"

Cathy leaned over the table. "Remember when I poured my guts out to you after I kicked Peter out? You can tell me anything."

"Lundh's got a mistress."

Cathy's eyes widened. "Lundh? Hasn't he been married to, what's her name?"

"Sharon. For over twenty years."

She shook her head. "You men are all alike, aren't you."

Richard looked into his coffee.

"Hey, I didn't mean you. You're just about the only decent guy I know. I'm just bitter, I guess. You know how long Peter was banging that bimbo of his? Almost a year. Right under my nose! You know how that feels?"

Richard gently grasped her hand. "Take it easy. Like you said before, all that's behind you now."

"I know, I know. Anyway, what do you plan to do—blow the whistle on him?"

"Something like that."

"Are you sure he's got a girlfriend?"

"Oh, he's got someone all right. Her name is Angela. She works in his office. About a year ago, before that whole committee mess, when we were still tennis buddies, Lundh and I were at a tennis tournament on Martha's Vineyard for the hospital's tennis club. I showed up early and caught the two of them kissing in the far corner of a parking lot. They didn't see me, but I recognized her. She's his billing person. She's been with him for years."

Cathy shrugged. "All that proves is that he's a prick. It could've been a one-time deal. It doesn't mean he's having an affair."

"Not so fast. When I was driving home from the party, I discovered I had his racquet instead of mine. I must have accidentally grabbed it in the locker room. Anyway, I was going to give him a call, but since I was going right by his development, I figured I'd drop by his place and make the switch."

Richard motioned to the approaching server for another round of coffees.

"As I came down his street, I saw him pull into his driveway. I was almost at his house when, to my great surprise, I saw a certain person get out of the passenger's side."

Cathy leaned forward. "Angela?"

"Yep. She hopped out of the car and looked around as if she owned the place."

"Lundh didn't see you?"

"Nope. I drove right past."

"In that conspicuous Jag?"

"No. I had the SUV, thank God."

"Where was his wife?"

"Who the hell knows? Not at home, I bet."

Cathy shrugged. "That was a year ago. How do you know—?"

"Hang on. A couple of months ago, before all this mess came down, I happened to see them both in the hospital parking lot when I was leaving. Lundh was going to his car. Angela seemed to be following him but trailed behind by, I don't know, about ten feet, I'd say. She got to his car just as he got in, hesitated a moment at his driver's side door, then turned around and walked to her car. They then drove off *together*. It was like he waited for her. I don't know. You had to see it. It looked kind of fishy."

Cathy finished her pastry. "Big deal. They left the parking lot together. I think you're seeing ghosts."

"Let me finish. So they pulled out, and I didn't give it another thought. But then, a few minutes later, I happen to spot them just ahead of me in heavy traffic, one behind the other, waiting at a light. The light turned green, she pulled into the next left turn lane, and I'll be damned if he didn't cozy right up behind her. A second later, I saw them turning off, down a small side street, just as I passed them."

She shrugged. "Maybe they were both just going home."

He shook his head. "Not even close. Lundh lives in the opposite direction. I've been to his house many times."

She swept some crumbs onto the floor. "What did you do then, turn around and follow them?"

"Of course not. I went home and forgot all about it. None of my business, I thought. But now, after what the bastard did to me . . ."

"But now it is your business?"

He looked into his coffee cup. "Maybe."

"So what are you going to do, tell his wife?"

Richard sat up and leaned forward, as if telling a secret. "I just hired a private detective."

"What for?"

He sat back and sighed. "Right now I'm not really sure. I had this idea, but . . ." He shook his head.

"What idea?"

"Lundh mentioned a few months ago that his wife was staying over at her ailing mother's house on Friday nights to help take care of her. I figured that could be a good time to catch them in the act."

"Catch them in the act?" She laughed. "What are you going to do, bug his house?"

Richard cleared his throat and studied the coffee cup before him. "That was the idea."

Cathy sat back and rubbed her neck. "Wow. I don't know, Richard. It sounds kind of crazy to me."

He shrugged. "It doesn't matter. It would cost too much money anyway. Something like seventy-five thousand bucks. So he's just going to follow Lundh outside, hoping he can catch them together, doing something."

"Like what? They're not kids anymore, you know. But you could still blow the whistle on him based on what you already know. I'm not sure about that letter, though. You don't want stuff like that in print."

Richard caught a glimpse of Cathy's hand resting on the table, her slender fingers inches away from his. An instant later, her hand disappeared into her lap.

"Yeah, well, at this point, I'm not sure what I'm going to do."

Cathy tapped her spoon on the table. "I don't know about your crazy ideas, but, between you and me, I hope you take that son of a bitch down somehow."

Richard smiled. "Me, too."

She looked at her watch. "I'm afraid I'd better be going. Time to treat myself to a hot bath and bed."

He paid the bill. "Thanks for listening to my troubles."

She smiled warmly and squeezed his hand. "Isn't that what friends are for? Keep in touch."

———〰〰———

Richard slid behind the wheel of his car and paused before putting the key into the ignition. His outpouring to Cathy had somehow left him feeling lighter, less burdened, more hopeful.

A few minutes later, he found Leslie sitting up in bed, pouring over a book on Salvador Dali.

"How was tennis?" she asked, keeping her head in the book.

Richard hesitated. "I . . . we didn't play. I don't feel so hot. Bit of a sore throat. We just sat at the bar and had a drink and talked. I told him about my problem."

Leslie looked up from her book. Richard looked away.

"Shouldn't you be keeping that stuff to yourself?"

"Why?" he asked, going into the bathroom.

"What did he say?"

"Same thing I've said to you. Something ain't right."

"Well, I'd be careful of who you talk to."

Richard emerged from the bathroom and crawled into bed. "I will." He kissed Leslie goodnight and rolled over.

For the next hour, he lay awake, silently cursing himself for his lie. He looked over at Leslie, fast asleep, her face buried in the covers.

He got up, went downstairs, and turned on the television.

Three nights later, after a quiet dinner with Leslie at home, Richard went into his office. The lingering guilt he had felt over his lie to her was finally starting to wane. He fell back into his chair and impatiently flipped through *The Professional's Comprehensive Manual on Surveillance*, barely glancing at the pages. He would race through it once, and then burn it.

Moments later, he began paying a little more attention. Before he knew it, he found himself hunched over the pages, his wide eyes devouring every detail, not stopping until he had worked his way through the entire manual. *Remote microphones, wireless microphones . . . processors . . . receivers . . . burst transmitters . . . frequency modulation . . . bullets . . . repeaters/blimp hangars . . . bugs . . . ground plane antennas . . . listening post . . . switches/loops/ POTS/PBX/DISA port . . . black market . . .*

Richard sat up and looked around the room, as if briefly forgetting where he was. He looked at the time and gasped. Almost three hours had flown by in an instant. He began to run his hand over the shiny cover, and then stopped abruptly.

The idea hit him like a lightning bolt. *I'll do it myself.*

He began pacing in the office, his brain a cacophony of noise and confusion.

Have I lost my mind?

He sat back down and glanced at the manual, waiting for outrage and guilt and even shame to flood through him, washing everything away.

Nothing happened.

He locked the book safely away in his desk drawer and headed out to the kitchen. For the first time in a week, he felt alive. Invisible hands had suddenly been wrenched from his neck. He could breathe again. He made a mental note to call off the private investigator in the morning.

He opened the basement door. He could hear Leslie working in her studio, humming to music from the Gipsy Kings, one of her favorites. He smiled and closed the door gently.

Better turn in early and get a good night's sleep.

He had his work cut out for him.

13

Richard hit the "end" button on his phone, sat back, and smiled. What a week he'd had. For the last three afternoons, he had sat in his car in the far corner of a busy shopping mall, armed with his phone, dog-eared surveillance manual, files, folders, books, magazines, and notepads, planning his grand surveillance operation. How many calls had he made? California, Texas, New York, Mexico, Germany, and finally, New Zealand. The work had been tedious and at times somewhat frustrating, but today had been a great day. He opened his window and breathed in the wonderful New England spring air.

Richard glanced at the clock. Three thirty. Time to pack up and head home. He placed his various pieces of scrap paper, articles, pamphlets, and little green book of telephone numbers into several large manila envelopes and hid them, together with the manual, in the hole next to the spare tire.

That afternoon, he had finally solved the one remaining troublesome issue. He had not yet worked out the manner in which he would obtain, copy, and safely return Lundh's house keys. Richard knew he could get it done on his own, but having an accomplice—he grimaced at the word—having a *partner* would make it so much easier, not to mention safer. The solution came to him in a flash.

Cathy.

Would she do it? Based on her response the other night at the café, he felt he had a chance. He dug out the tiny scrap of paper in his wallet where he had scribbled down her cell number.

"Hello, Cathy?"

"Who is this?"

"It's Richard. How are you?"

"Oh, I'm sorry, Richard. I didn't recognize the number. I'm fine. How are you?"

"I'm fine. I was wondering if I could meet you somewhere, just for a moment."

"Let me guess: Lundh."

"Bingo."

"Let's see . . . Why don't you come over this Monday evening, to my place, around seven."

"Sounds great. I'll see you then. Call me at this number if something comes up."

"Got it. See you Monday."

Richard opened his sunroof and headed for home.

14

The following Monday, Richard sat at the dinner table, his stomach tied in knots. He tried to enjoy the meal, but all he could think about was meeting Cathy. Justin left the table early to call a friend, leaving Leslie and Richard alone with their dessert. He couldn't wait any longer.

"I was thinking of going down to the club tonight for a little tennis. I'll be back around nine thirty. Maybe we could watch a movie."

Leslie poked at her strawberry ice cream. "Okay."

Justin returned from his bedroom. "Hey, Mom, can I go to the Bruins game tonight with David and his dad?"

"Sure, sweetheart. What time can I expect you back?"

"About eleven."

"Be careful. Have fun."

Leslie sighed. "You know, I can remember a time when he'd be so excited to go with you to a game. You guys used to have such fun. You were his best friend. These days, he acts as if you don't even exist."

Richard picked up his coffee, and then slowly lowered the cup to the table without taking a sip. He stood up, walked toward the window over the sink, and looked outside at the trees. A moment later, he felt a gentle tap on his shoulder.

"The sad thing is, you miss your boy. I can tell. You should see your face every time he sees you without saying hello, or barks at you, or finds some bullshit excuse to avoid going out with you somewhere. I know how hard you tried to do things with him last summer, but now it looks like you've just given up. Maybe if you take an afternoon off here and there, you know, make yourself a little more available . . ."

Richard turned toward her. "I'll try to do better, Les. I promise."

"I know you will, dear." Leslie smiled. "Go on, have some fun tonight. I'll see you later."

Richard set out for Cathy's house about six thirty, still stinging from Leslie's comments. He turned on the radio and immediately shut it off. He suddenly yearned to tell Leslie everything. How he wished she would embrace his plans and offer to help. Last night, after one too many glasses of Merlot, he had come within a breath of telling her. Fortunately, he had saved himself in the nick of time. She would have ripped him to pieces.

He stepped on the gas.

Magnificent oak and elm trees lined the winding country road. A misty drizzle fell. Richard loved the rain. He opened his window just enough to hear the wonderful sound his tires made as he drove down the winding country road.

Cathy's house was a luxurious, red-brick colonial with massive columns, shuttered windows, and a second-story balcony. She answered the door in snug designer jeans and a sleeveless, cream-colored silk blouse. Her shoulder-length brown hair was tied back in a ponytail, exposing her smooth, slender neckline.

"Hi there. Wow. I hope you didn't get dressed up just for me."

She smiled. "No. I'm meeting my sister and her husband in Cambridge for drinks. I'll need to leave about nine, if that's okay."

He glanced at his watch. "Nine?"

"I'm sorry. She called me early this evening. We've still got a couple of hours."

Cathy disappeared into the kitchen, came back with two glasses of wine, and sat next to Richard in front of the fireplace. She tasted the wine and gave him a warm smile.

"Has the PI come up with anything?"

"Not a thing. I told him to forget it; I was just wasting his time."

"Maybe so, but you haven't really given him a chance, have you?"

"I've got a much better idea."

Cathy frowned and pulled back slightly.

Richard laughed. "Don't worry, it's nothing like that. Listen, I've been looking at this book on surveillance. I'm telling you, Cathy, I couldn't believe my eyes."

"What the hell are you talking about?"

"What I'm talking about is, I can do this. Myself, I mean."

"You can do what, the bugging?

"Yes, the bugging, if you must use that term."

"What else do you want me to call it?"

Richard rubbed his eyes and sighed.

"You're really serious about this, aren't you?"

"Yes, I am."

"You do realize this little scheme of yours is illegal?"

Richard looked into his lap.

Cathy rose. "Why are you telling me all this?"

"Jack's wife is going out of town for her niece's wedding in nine weeks. I overheard him in the lunchroom. I wouldn't have remembered the date, except that it happens to be the same day I had planned to host a symposium here in town. The symposium was cancelled, but the date stuck in my mind."

Cathy shook her head. "I don't know what to say. I mean, I agree he's got it coming. But bugging his house? I don't know."

"Don't you see? It's a golden opportunity."

"To get yourself in a mess of trouble. Anyway, why tell me?"

Richard stepped toward her and grasped her hand. "I need your help."

Cathy pulled back. "What?"

"You know that part I told you about where I get his keys out of his locker in the surgeon's locker room? Well, I figured out a way to get it done myself, but . . ."

"Jesus, you're not going to ask me to get the keys."

"No. All I need you to do is to *copy* his keys. That's it. The whole thing should take only about an hour of your time."

"Copy his keys?"

"I have to get in to install the surveillance equipment."

"You've got to be kidding me."

"On Tuesday mornings, from seven until at least two, Lundh is in the OR."

"Doesn't he lock his locker?"

"Nobody does. You just take your wallet with you into the

OR. Who the hell is interested in stealing your clothes, or keys, for that matter?"

Cathy looked at her watch.

"As you know," he continued, "we just happen to have that little park across the street. While he's in surgery, I'm going to grab his keys. I'll put his house key in an envelope and put it in a squirrel hole in the large oak tree about twenty feet from the park bench across the street. It's easy to find, and no one would notice it. The tree is partly hidden by the stone monument, and the squirrel hole is deep."

Cathy shook her head firmly. "Jesus, Richard."

"All you have to do is be in the park right before nine. Wait about two minutes after I've gone back in the hospital, then pick up the keys, get them copied, and return them in the same envelope to the tree. The key place is just a mile east on Delorme Avenue, same side as the park. I've checked, and it's not very busy that time of day. It shouldn't take more than a half an hour.

"What if Lundh has an alarm system?"

"If he does, he doesn't use it during the day. Before all this came down with the QA thing, I would occasionally pick him up at his office in the afternoon for tennis. I remember once when we were headed out the front door, his hands were full, and he asked me to make sure the door was locked. I asked him if he needed to activate a security system, and he said he didn't use one."

"Why don't you just copy them yourself, maybe during your lunch hour or something?"

"I need to make sure the keys are replaced before he's done in the OR. Sometimes, he finishes before me. Most of my cases are from out of town, some even out of state, scheduled months ahead. I wouldn't feel good about messing with that. Besides, staying busy and accounted for is part of my alibi, if it ever came to that, which I seriously doubt."

Cathy walked over to a black-and-white Ansel Adams print of Yosemite National Park hanging above the fireplace mantle.

"Cathy, I can't even begin to tell you how much it would mean to me if you could help me with this. I promise you, it'll be the last thing I'll ask you to do. You know me—no strings attached, I promise."

She turned toward him and opened her mouth to speak, but then closed it.

"Come on," he said. "You can't deny I've been brutalized by that bastard. You know he's got it coming to him, not only from me, but his wife, as well."

Cathy walked away into the kitchen. Richard waited, quiet and still. After about a minute, she emerged, a crease in her brow, rubbing her eyes. "Yeah, okay, I'll do it. I guess."

Richard forcefully exhaled. "From the bottom of my heart, I thank you."

"I must be out of my mind."

Richard glanced at his watch. "I'd better let you go. I'll give you a call in the next day or two to go over the details."

"Before you leave, I do have one question."

"Of course, anything."

"Have you spoken to Leslie about this?"

Richard looked away. "No. I didn't."

"Listen Richard, if I'm going to help you with this scheme of yours, you're going to have to be straight with me on a few things."

He turned toward her. "Believe me, Cathy, I would have liked nothing more than to tell her and have her understand and help me. But here I am, pouring my guts out to you. And you know why? Because for some crazy reason, I happen to think that you're just about the only person on the face of this earth who might understand my misery and be willing to take a chance to help me. Tell me now if you don't think you can be that person, and I'll just leave and forget we ever had this conversation."

Cathy buried her face in her hands. "No. I told you. I'll help you."

"Are you sure?"

She nodded. "Yes. You can count on me. That number you gave me . . . is it private?"

"Yeah. It's one of those prepaid cell phones. I'm using it for all calls related to this, just to be safe."

She shook her head and sighed. "Okay, get out of here. I've got to go."

Richard felt a surge of adrenaline as he walked down the driveway. Cathy had, however reluctantly, agreed to help him. Like a starving child crying out for food, he felt nothing could have been more richly satisfying. He got into his car, turned on some music, and drove home.

Two nights later, Richard sat at his desk in his home office, enjoying a glass of his favorite Merlot. He couldn't imagine being anywhere else in the world. This wonderful room, tucked away in the back of the house, was his personal hideout. He glanced at the beautiful watercolor of a farmhouse painted by Leslie and a photograph of the family hiking on the Appalachian Trail several years ago.

The house was empty. Leslie was away at her painting workshop. He turned out the lights in his office, walked to the window, and gazed at his favorite tree, a massive old elm, now in early bloom, silhouetted by garden spotlights.

What joy he had felt sharing his story with Cathy. He wished her response had been more enthusiastic, but her reluctance was understandable. She had agreed to support and help him; that was what mattered. He still wished it could have been Leslie.

The clock on the wall chimed ten. Leslie would be back soon. He strolled to the kitchen for a bite to eat. As usual, on evenings when she was out, he had ordered pizza for himself and Justin. He helped himself to a small slice when the front door flew open. Leslie burst into the kitchen.

"I think I may have done it! Remember that surrealist

painter from San Francisco I was telling you about a few months ago? The guy I showed you in the magazine?"

"Sure. I remember how excited you were."

Justin came into the kitchen and headed straight to the pizza box.

"Hi, Mom." He paused to swallow a bite of cold pizza. "How was your workshop?"

"Fantastic. I met James Retne tonight at Margo's."

"Isn't that the guy in the magazine?"

"Yeah, yeah, that's him. Margo showed him a few of my best works at the studio, and guess what? He was impressed."

Richard raised his eyebrows. "Wow. That's great! Congratulations, honey."

"Wait, that's not even the best part. He asked my permission to talk to a few galleries in Boston and Chicago, to maybe get me a decent gallery showing somewhere. Can you believe that? He also wants to see more of my work here at home!"

Justin stepped in front of his father. "Sounds like this could finally be your big break, Mom."

Leslie threw her head back and shut her eyes. "God, I hope so."

Richard patted his son on the back.

"We're both really happy for you, Les."

"Good job, Mom. I knew you could do it." Justin kissed her, and then headed for the stairs.

Leslie tossed the pizza box into the refrigerator. "Hey, that was really nice to see."

"What?"

"You and Justin, together like that. For a second, we were like a real family."

Richard shrugged. "Hey, I'm trying."

"I know you are, dear. Anyway, what a night. I think I'll soak in the tub and rest my happy, weary bones." She wrapped her arms around his waist and caressed his lips with her tongue. "Want to join me?"

He flashed a grin. "Try to stop me."

Go on; make love to her. Celebrate her success. Who knows, you might somehow find the courage to tell her.

Richard flipped off the kitchen light and sprinted up the stairs behind her.

16

For the next few days, Richard struggled to stay focused on his usual activities, but his upcoming scheme was never far from his mind. The following Monday, the eve of the operation, he placed a call from his "secret line" while going home from work through a driving rain.

"Hello Cathy? It's Richard. How are you?"

"I'm fine."

"Are we good, I mean, for tomorrow?"

She remained silent.

"Cathy, are you okay?"

"Yeah, everything's fine. I'm ready to go."

"Great. I'll call you after it's over."

As he ended the call, he couldn't help but wonder: was she really fine?

At six thirty the next morning, Richard's alarm clock blasted to life. The life-altering significance of the hours that lay ahead tightened his muscles. He kissed Leslie on the forehead. On any other Tuesday morning, he would have hit the snooze button a few times before dragging himself into the shower. But this was not just another day.

He shaved, showered, and dressed with shaking hands and a churning stomach. Leslie remained asleep, curled up in her usual fetal position with the covers pulled up over her nose. Ringlets of golden-blond hair hid most of her face. He gently moved a few locks aside and gave her a light kiss on her cheek.

Wish me luck, darling.

At seven thirty, Richard started his first procedure on a middle-aged man with chronic alcoholic pancreatitis. The case required endoscopic placement of a pancreatic stent, which, together with alcohol abstinence and acid suppression, may reduce pain. A number of other gastroenterologists in the greater Boston area also performed this procedure, but Richard had the most experience and lowest complication rate.

He finished the case by 8:25. As luck would have it, Lundh's first case was an abdominal aortic aneurysm, something that would keep him occupied until at least noon.

Richard slipped into the men's locker room, checked around, and peeked inside the bathroom. He was alone. He put on a latex glove and was just about to open Lundh's locker when he heard several people enter the lounge. He hid in one of the bathroom stalls before they came into the locker room. His heart pounded as if it were about to jump out of his chest. He glanced at his watch—8:35.

Just stay calm.

Locker doors flew open and clanged shut. The handle to his stall door suddenly shook. He threw his hand up to the door.

"Ah, just a minute, please."

To his great relief, the person left the locker room. Moments later, Richard slipped on his gloves, emerged from the stall, and opened Lundh's locker door. He delicately removed Lundh's keys lying on the bottom of the locker, eased the door closed, and ran back into the bathroom soaking in sweat.

He removed his gloves, wiped his face on his shirtsleeve, and threw the key chain into his pocket. He took a deep breath and checked his watch—8:39. Time had suddenly become an issue. He opened the door a crack and listened. Hearing nothing, he strode swiftly into the short hall connecting the endoscopy and OR suites. He practically ran into one of the endoscopy nurses.

"There you are, Doc. We'll be ready in five. Tough IV."

"Take your time. I'm going to go get some coffee in the doctor's lunchroom. That OR stuff is dreadful."

Oh God, did I look suspicious?

He found a bathroom on the other side of the hospital and examined the keys. Of the five on the ring, he removed the two that looked like candidates for the front door. He raced across the street to the small, secluded park with the big, beautiful trees. He checked the time—8:44. A young woman with a child sat on the park bench. He looked frantically around.

Where the hell is she?

His stomach tightened. A horrific constellation of worst-case scenarios flooded his mind. Had she had a last-minute change of heart? Had Lundh discovered the theft? Had somebody seen him and informed Lundh? Had the police been called? Was his career over?

He placed the envelope with the keys into the hollow knot of the tree and took one final look around. He still didn't see her. He hurried back to the hospital, taking a rarely used side entrance. At 8:48, he arrived at the endoscopy suite.

He greeted his next patient, a middle-aged, jaundiced woman, with a reassuring smile. Shortly after beginning the procedure, he became aware of the large key chain rubbing against the inside of his left leg. The notion of having anything handled by Lundh next to his body made him shudder. He would rather have had a dead rat in his pocket. But where else could he have safely hidden the keys? He cleared his mind and cannulated the patient's common bile duct.

At eleven thirty, he finished an unusually difficult procedure on a patient with large, common, bile-duct stones. He took his usual fifteen-minute break for a granola bar and coffee. What if she hadn't shown? He would have to return the keys to the locker, but then what? Time to find out.

He took the same careful route back to the park. He scanned the area. Nobody in sight. He headed straight for the tree, his forehead soaked in sweat. He took one final look around, took a deep breath, and peeked into the hollow knot.

The envelope was in the exact position in which he'd left it. His heart sank. He snatched it out of the knot and was about to jam it into his pocket when he froze. It felt heavier.

With trembling hands, he ripped open the envelope. Four keys flew onto the sidewalk. Sweet Jesus, what a beautiful sight lay before him—the two originals with two perfect copies. He gathered up his prize and hustled back to the hospital. He put the originals on the key chain exactly in the order they had been previously, sauntered casually into the locker room, and replaced the keys on the floor of Lundh's locker in the original position.

Mission accomplished.

Richard completed his afternoon teaching rounds and arrived back at the office a little after five. He looked out at his trees. How did he feel? He wasn't sure. He had tried to prepare himself for a stressful ordeal, but he had no idea how tough this would turn out to be. He felt relief, but where was that feeling of euphoria he had so eagerly anticipated?

He had never done anything illegal before.

Stop it! Have you already forgotten what that bastard Lundh did to you?

How wonderful Cathy had been to help him. He couldn't wait to thank her. Perhaps he would send her flowers.

Richard lifted his weary body out of the chair and headed home. If the traffic wasn't too terrible, he might make it in time for dinner with Leslie and Justin.

Cathy pulled into her driveway at about noon, still shaken from the events of the morning. Fortunately her physician assistant was able to see her afternoon appointments. She collapsed onto her couch and closed her eyes.

I can't believe what I just did.

She dragged herself into the shower. Perhaps she could wash all the frightful uneasiness down the drain.

Cheating son of a bitch deserves it, doesn't he?

She ran a comb through her wet hair, tied it back, and looked at her naked body in the mirror. She worked hard to keep her slender frame in its youthful form. The skin of her face and neck was still relatively wrinkle-free. Her moderate sized breasts certainly weren't those of her youth, but they still looked reasonably perky for forty-five. All in all, she was pleased with her appearance. If only she felt as good as she looked.

She threw on her bathrobe, popped some leftovers into the microwave, and poured herself an iced tea. She would try to relax and decompress, maybe read a book, or perhaps watch a movie.

She was about to take the first bite of her lasagna when the doorbell rang. She peered through the peephole and found a young man with flowers.

"Who is it?"

"Florist delivery for Miss Wilcox."

Cathy accepted the delivery of two dozen, long-stemmed pink roses in a tall crystal vase. She placed them on her coffee table, leaned over the beautiful arrangement, and inhaled. She spotted a small envelope amongst the stems.

"Ouch!"

A tiny drop of blood appeared on the tip of her finger. She opened the envelope—*Thanks for everything.* She wiped off the blood with a tissue, called Richard's private cell phone, and left a voicemail thanking him for his kindness.

After finishing her lunch, she decided she would settle in with her book. She sat on the couch with a glass of wine and tried to read, but couldn't concentrate. She looked at the roses and thought about Richard. A moment later, she pulled up an internet site on roses. Pink roses stood for appreciation, gratitude.

She smiled. Lundh had it coming to him anyway. All she did was copy keys. She would consider this her token act of defiance to all the lying, cheating men of the world.

A warm euphoria began to engulf her. She took another large sip of wine and closed her eyes.

An hour later, her cell phone jolted her awake.

"Hi, Cathy. It's me, Richard. How are you?"

"Hi. I'm fine, I guess. Thanks for the roses. You didn't have to do that."

"I just wanted to thank you for your help. I knew you'd come through. When I saw those keys . . . I can't even begin to thank you."

"Yeah, well, I just hope you don't do anything too crazy."

"Don't worry. Anyway, I just wanted to let you know I really appreciate what you did for me. Take care. I'll talk to you soon."

Appreciation without strings felt good. No sexual advances, no hidden agendas, no deceit. He could have sent red roses. He was just an honest guy who got royally screwed by a real asshole.

Still, wasn't he going a little too far? Mind you, Lundh hadn't ripped her guts out. She tried to imagine what she would have done. She knew as well as anyone that rage can make you do crazy things.

She grabbed her book and headed for the couch.

For the next several weeks, Richard immersed himself in his work—seeing patients, doing procedures, discussing cases with his partners, and carrying out his teaching duties at the hospital. Damned if he'd allow this whole nasty business to contaminate the work he loved.

He checked his desk calendar. In two days, Lundh would be flying to Atlanta for the American College of Surgery meeting, an event he attended every year without fail, or so he had stated in a letter to the QA committee. A few discreet telephone calls last week had confirmed Lundh's registration for this year's two-day meeting.

Richard awoke early on the morning of the big day. He began his drive to Logan Airport just as dawn broke. Thirty minutes later, he crept up the ramp to Departing Flights and parked about a hundred feet in front of the drop-off area for Delta. Fortunately, the traffic was heavy, allowing him to blend in easily. He slid down in his seat, waited, and watched.

Fifteen minutes later, Lundh's Mercedes pulled up to the valet parking ahead of him. The contemptible bastard emerged, passed through the curbside check-in, and with his one carry-on bag, disappeared into the airport. Richard turned on some music and drove off.

On the way to work, he called Delta and was reassured that the flight to Atlanta had left on time. At ten thirty, he called again and made sure of the flight's arrival. A needless step, perhaps, but one could never be too careful.

At noon, Richard drove to the Cumberland mall with a loaner BMW SUV he had secured the previous night, after dropping off his Jaguar at the dealer for routine service. The Jag might attract unnecessary attention.

In a corner of the mall parking lot, he changed clothes, added a moustache—he felt ridiculous doing this—threw on a hat, and checked his supplies: video camera, tape measure, pen and paper, two prepaid phones with hands-free earpieces, and, of course, the house keys.

His first step would be to ensure that Lundh's wife, Sharon, was at work and would remain there for the duration. Her clothing boutique was located among a small cluster of fashionable stores about three miles from their home. Richard found her Acura sedan. Fortunately, it was parked away from the storefront.

Time for a test run. He activated both of his phones, giving each phone three hours of uninterrupted airtime. Street noise came through loud and clear on both phones. He placed one phone in his pocket, and carefully placed the other in a bubble-padded bag. He parked next to the Acura, discreetly placed the phone under the inside half of Sharon's passenger side front tire, and hopped back into his car. He plugged in his earphone. *Voila!* A background of car engines producing a meaningless dissonance filled Richard's ear. As long as he heard this, he was safe.

Thirty minutes later, Richard pulled up to a small, brick

gatehouse. He had the option of following the car of a resident through the open gate, but instead, he chose to stay with his plan. He addressed the gatekeeper with a pleasant smile.

"Good afternoon. I'd like to visit the model homes."

An elderly man with thick white hair, wearing a dark blue uniform, reached for his clipboard. "Certainly, sir. Do you have an appointment?"

"No, I don't. Do I need one?"

This was more discussion than Richard wanted, but he kept his cool. He knew appointments weren't necessary.

"Oh, no, not at all. Have a good day."

Richard briefly visited two different models, making sure to be seen by the salespeople. Fifteen minutes later, he turned onto Lundh's street. He chose his parking spot carefully, two houses down. If nosy neighbors noticed his BMW, they wouldn't know which house was being visited. He checked his fake mustache in the rearview mirror. Sweat glistened on his chin and forehead. His phone continued to send him the muffled drone of traffic. He slipped his video camera into a large jacket pocket and put on his gloves. His hand froze on the car door handle.

Calm down. You'll be fine.

He strode toward the house with brisk steps and rang the bell. He kept his eyes focused on the door, resisting a temptation to look over his shoulder. He counted to thirty and rang again. Surely a cleaning lady would have answered by now. He took a deep breath, discreetly reached into his pocket for one of the two keys, and, with a gloved hand, tried the lock. The key fit snugly into the chamber. He held his breath and turned the key. The chamber smoothly rotated. He depressed the latch, pushed open the door, and entered. He spotted the alarm box on the wall, and held his breath. His heart pounded.

The alarm box remained silent. He exhaled. He had done it; he was in.

He walked quickly through the foyer and entered the spacious living room on the front right corner of the house. The early afternoon sun generously lit the room. He stood in the middle of the room and saw two options for surveillance— one from a DVD player three feet off the floor below a wide-screen television; the other from a grate in the ceiling in the middle of the room.

Richard took a close-up shot of both the DVD and the grate, and he measured the dimensions of the grate. Which was a better location? No time to worry about that now. He would look at the video later.

The kitchen had undergone changes since his last visit several years ago. Lundh had upgraded with cherry cabinets, a granite island and countertops, and a wide-plank oak floor. Richard spotted a large clock on the countertop in a corner of the kitchen. He wrote down the name and model of the clock and carefully replaced it.

The master bedroom revealed a four-post, king-sized bed covered with a purple-and-gold duvet. Richard's eyes fell upon a large grate in the ceiling near the wall facing the foot of the bed. Forget the rest of the house. This was perfect.

He glanced at his watch. He had been inside less than ten minutes. The master bath, complete with large tub, was also endowed with a usable ceiling vent.

Richard double-checked his supplies. The distant drone of traffic continued to sing in his ear. He checked the front of the house through the window. There was no one in sight. He locked the door and strode back to the car, his heart pumping wildly. Sweat soaked his face.

For a few moments, he sat in the car with the air conditioning blasting, trying to gather himself. How he wished Leslie could have been here. He glanced at his watch. Not bad—only a few minutes behind schedule.

He pulled out and started back for the office.

19

That night, Richard enjoyed a quiet dinner at home with Leslie.

"How's your painting going these days, sweetheart?"

"Oh fine. Actually, I'm doing more studying and less painting lately. I can't stop thinking of Dali. What a brilliant madman he was."

Richard laughed. "You think? What would *he* say to that?" He jumped up and cleared the table, humming a jazz tune.

Leslie smiled. "You're in an awfully good mood."

Richard grinned. "You might say that."

Leslie got up from the table, stretched, and grabbed her purse. "I need to run over to the pharmacy before it closes. Need anything?"

"No thanks."

The moment he heard the garage door close, Richard hurried into his office and found the remote control. Jack's house flashed onto the wide-screen television.

Oh, God, if Leslie ever catches me . . .

He meticulously studied the footage. His preliminary choices were confirmed. He would install his bugs in the family room DVD player, the kitchen clock, and the vent in the bedroom.

He unlocked his office drawer and extracted a large file labeled "Surveillance." His research had told him that he could easily acquire all the equipment in the United States, with one major exception. The receiver he needed, used only by government and law enforcement, could only be obtained overseas. He had then found a surveillance outlet in New Zealand that had all the goodies he wanted, including his precious receiver, which they would ship to anywhere in the United States within seven days. He retrieved the surveillance outlet phone number from the file and strolled into the kitchen just as Leslie's headlights swept across the living room.

—⚹—

The following Saturday morning, Richard began in earnest.

"Hey Les, I need to go into the office for a few hours to clean a few things up."

Leslie refilled his coffee. "What about our bike ride?"

"We can go the minute I get back. I won't be long."

As he pulled out of the driveway, he cursed himself. If only he didn't have to lie to her.

He purchased the bedroom air vent cover at a local hardware store, the DVD player from an electronics outlet, and the rosewood clock from a nearby specialty shop. He made all purchases with cash.

Finally, he was ready to place his order. Local time in Christchurch, New Zealand—late Sunday morning. Total cost: forty-eight hundred dollars. Estimated delivery date: nine days. Richard ended the call with a trembling finger. He sent a money order by overnight delivery and drove home. The following afternoon, he confirmed receipt of payment and was told the goods would be shipped the following day.

The night before Lundh's return, Richard didn't fall asleep for hours. Could he have accidentally left behind any clues? Could a neighbor have seen him? Could he have moved something that might have aroused suspicion? Or even worse, had he unwittingly committed a major gaffe that would identify him at the scene of the crime?

On Monday morning, Richard sat bolt upright in bed, his sleep-deprived mind already filled with Lundh. He drove to the hospital in a sweat. What if he ran into the bastard? At the hospital, he avoided the doctor's lounge, library, medical records, cafeteria, and even the bathrooms. At one o'clock, he fled the hospital thinking he was home free, only to spot Lundh from a distance in the doctor's parking lot. He momentarily froze in his tracks, and then sprinted to his car, keeping his head down, cursing under his breath.

The following Saturday morning, Richard headed out to Providence, Rhode Island, to deliver a lecture at an international conference on advanced therapeutic endoscopy techniques. He gave his lecture at ten, stayed for the question-and-answer session following the set of morning lectures, had lunch with several of the other professors at noon, and was back in his car by one.

He pulled up to the mail-drop store in the middle of a large strip mall on the outskirts of Providence. He retrieved the notice indicating his packages had arrived, handed the paper to the lady at the counter, and forced a smile. He couldn't help thinking that an FBI agent already knew about this. He thought at any second, an agent would leap up from behind the counter and arrest him at gunpoint. He braced himself for the worst. A moment later, a young man appeared from the back of the store with several large packages wrapped in plain brown paper. Richard piled the boxes onto a dolly, signed his false name, and closed out his mailbox account.

He drove for about a mile, and then pulled over to the side of the road. He reached into the back seat, grabbed one of the parcels, and with trembling fingers, ripped it open.

His wide-open, disbelieving eyes stared at the bullet

camera. He frantically opened the other packages. Everything had been delivered.

On the way home, Richard made a reservation at Leslie's favorite Italian restaurant. He pulled into his driveway at six thirty, right on schedule. He felt like a criminal. Yet, at the same time, his insides churned and roiled with an even stronger feeling he could neither describe nor, for that matter, control. Maybe after a few drinks, he would find the courage to tell Leslie.

If only she could understand.

Four nights later, while Leslie was out with a group of friends, Richard hauled all his new gear, an extension cord, power bar, and a cup of tea into the attic. He attached the infrared bullet cameras onto the inside surface of the vent covers, carefully adjusting the slat angles to optimize viewing. He drilled a four-millimeter hole through the base of the clock, careful to avoid splintering, and attached the pinhole camera. He secured another pinhole camera inside the DVD player with ease. Finally he unpacked the superstar of the team: the expensive, legal-to-import-but-illegal-to-operate brain of the system—the audio/video receiver.

Richard sat back on a wood beam and took a deep breath. Twenty-three days and that crucial Friday night at the Lundh residence would be upon him. Twenty-three more days and he could finally start to breathe again.

Justice.

And so Richard waited. From the vantage point of the world around him, all must have appeared well. But inside, he writhed and boiled, counting the minutes.

On Thursday, one day before *the* day, Richard placed a confirmation call to Boutique Coco in the late afternoon.

"Hello, may I speak to Mrs. Lundh?"

"I'm afraid she's not in today."

"Oh, I see. She asked me to call this week to check on an order I'd placed for my wife."

"She'll be back on Monday. Can I be of assistance?"

"Oh, that's right. She's in Jacksonville for her sister's wedding, isn't she?"

"That's right. She left yesterday. Perhaps I can help? What's your wife's name?"

"No, no. Sorry to trouble you. I'll call back Monday. Thank you."

Richard returned from his early Friday morning jog feeling both excited and terrified. Leslie lay curled up on her left side, her face hidden by hair and covers. He gently slipped the covers below her chin, brushed away a few curly strands of hair, and gave her a light kiss on the nose.

Forgive me, darling.

At eleven o'clock, Richard left his office for a routine appointment with his own primary care physician. He activated both of his two prepaid phones in the doctor's parking lot and placed one of them under Lundh's front passenger side tire.

He was found to be in good health, other than mild hypertension. He got into his car, started the engine, took a deep breath, and drove off.

The guard at the gatehouse smiled. "Good morning, sir. How can I help you?"

"Good morning. I'm here to see the models."

This time Richard drove directly to Lundh's street, parking in his previous spot. He wore a navy pinstripe suit and pulled a large suitcase on wheels. Each footstep pounded in his ears for all to hear. Surely someone was peering at him now. What if a police car came screaming down the street?

Finally, he reached the front step. He glanced over his shoulder. Nobody around. He rang the bell and waited for what seemed like an eternity. No answer. In a flash, he hid his precious signal repeater in the bushes below the front window, eased the door open, and leapt inside.

Richard began with the DVD player. He gently pulled the small entertainment center away from the wall and made the switch. The removal and reattachment of the cables took him only a few seconds. He reinserted a DVD he found in Lundh's unit into his replacement unit and made sure the remote functioned.

Next, he turned his attention to the kitchen clock. Within seconds he made the switch, set the clock, and made sure it was working. The time on the clock showed he had been inside for just eleven minutes.

In the bedroom, Richard popped out the air vent with his cordless power screwdriver and had the modified one in place within minutes. The new vent didn't fit precisely, but he was able to muscle it into place. Now to activate the unit while staying out of view.

He ran down the stairs and headed for the front door, but was stopped by a thunderously loud chorus of chimes just as he entered the foyer. He stood frozen on dead legs, hands shaking, soaking in sweat.

Wait a second. This couldn't be Lundh; he wouldn't be ringing his own doorbell. Besides, his phone continued to give him a reassuring hum. Richard crept toward the door, held his breath, and looked through the peephole. The top half of a little girl, dressed in a Girl Scout's uniform, caught his eye. He crept quietly into the kitchen and waited several minutes in absolute silence before looking again. When he peeked, she was gone. He quietly opened the door, locked it, and left with the suitcase in tow. He drove past the gatehouse, barely able to see, overcome with terror and exhilaration. He drove into a secluded park, pulled into his usual spot tucked away in a far corner under a magnificent maple, and collapsed onto his steering wheel.

Oh God, I really did it.

Celebrate, damn you, celebrate!

His mind traveled back to that dreaded phone call, the visit to McAllister, and Sharkey's revelations. He pictured the new ambulatory center, Lundh as the medical director. He imagined the physician community wondering why Chase hadn't been invited to join the party. He could almost see that contemptuous bastard gloating over his triumph.

Damn you! You drove me to this, you bastard.

Richard wiped the sweat off his face and drove back to the office, in plenty of time for his three o'clock clinic.

21

That evening, Richard arrived home with his briefcase in one hand and Chinese food in the other. He would have about a half hour to eat a light dinner before his "tennis match" with Victor at eight.

He fumbled with his chopsticks over a plate of broccoli and chicken. "Are we still on for tomorrow night at Donatello's?"

"Sure. Are you trying to get me fat? Maybe I should go play some tennis with you."

He stiffened. "Okay. Maybe Sunday or something."

Richard threw his tennis gear into his back seat and fell behind the wheel. Would the lying never end? He wanted to run back into the house, tell her everything, beg for her understanding, and take his chances.

Just hang on a little longer. It'll soon be over.

He pulled into the far corner of the mall parking lot, hooked up the equipment, and inserted a disc into the DVD recorder. Tiny green lights on each of the units indicated power delivery. Any pixel change in the image caused by video activity would turn on both audio and video functions. He couldn't pick up audio outside the video range, but he could live with that.

Richard took a taxi to Lundh's development, getting out close to the unmanned back gate. He slipped under the gate and came to the vacant lot across the street from Lundh's house. The driveway was empty, and the lights were out. Eight fifteen. He settled behind a large maple tree and waited.

Dusk quickly gave way to darkness. Before he knew it, it was nine o'clock. Was it possible Lundh and his mistress wouldn't be getting together tonight? He had counted on them taking advantage of this golden opportunity.

Minutes became hours. Could they have gone to her house for the night? Impossible. His research had revealed that an old woman in a wheelchair, probably Angela's mother, lived with her. So where the hell were they?

Richard looked down at his watch. Ten o'clock. Still nothing. He was just thinking what a colossal waste of time he'd spent when the blue Mercedes approached the house and pulled into the driveway. The garage door opened, and the car pulled inside. He saw the silhouette of Lundh step out of the driver's side. Richard held his breath and looked at the passenger side as the garage door slowly closed.

The passenger door didn't open.

Richard walked away from the cover of the tree, his head lowered. He walked to a convenience store outside Lundh's development, called a taxi, and rode back to the mall in silence. He flopped down behind the wheel and buried his face in his hands. He started the car, but suddenly realized he couldn't just drive home with his vehicle looking like a television studio. The idea of tearing it all down seemed unbearable. At least he could try again tomorrow and Sunday night. They had to be getting together sometime.

A cough, partially cut off, caught his attention. Richard turned to look at the screen. Nothing. He was about to turn away when the kitchen monitor lit up, showing a remarkably clear image of Lundh standing next to the refrigerator. The technical accomplishment was lost on Richard. The sight of Lundh turned his stomach.

"What can I get you to drink?" Lundh asked, the words as clear as if Richard had been there himself.

The family room lit up, showing Angela, wearing a knee-length pencil skirt, blouse, and scarf, walking toward the couch. "Gin and tonic is fine," she said.

Richard caught his breath. He got out of the car and stared at the surveillance equipment through the window, dumbfounded, adrenaline rushing as if he had just run a marathon. He ran to the coffee shop in the plaza to steady his nerves. He had wanted to stay and watch more, but for some reason, he couldn't. The whole thing now seemed to happen so fast. For the first time he could remember, he didn't know what to think or do.

After about an hour of staring at a cup of coffee and wringing his hands, he went back to his car. Fortunately, the parking lot was still full from movie patrons in the multiplex.

He took a deep breath, turned his head, and looked at the screen. The scene he had hoped for, the scene that would make all the risk and blood and sweat worthwhile, now flashed before his eyes. He got out of the car and pumped his fist in the night air.

An hour later, Richard returned from a brisk walk in the neighborhood next to the mall and rechecked the screen. Blank. He dismantled his equipment, packed it up in the trunk, and drove away, barely able to sit still.

He arrived home at about one thirty and fell into bed a few

minutes later, exhausted. Leslie was sound asleep. He kissed her shoulder and gently shook her.

"Sweetheart, I'm back."

"Huh? What time is it?"

"About one. I had a drink at the club."

"You win?"

"Win?" He cleared his throat. "Yes. You could say that."

He rolled over, closed his eyes, and waited for sleep.

Saturday crept by with agonizing slowness. Richard wanted desperately to watch the recording, but promised himself he would wait until he spoke to Cathy. He was hoping they could view it together at her place. He also needed to dispose of the electronics equipment, now safely tucked away in the attic, but he needn't worry about that now.

That evening, he and Leslie headed out to their favorite restaurant. On the drive over, he placed his hand on her exposed thigh. "Is that a new dress? Looks nice."

Leslie laughed. "I've had it for a while, but thanks for noticing."

After dessert, they wandered over to the lounge, sat at their usual table next to the piano, and ordered brandies. He squeezed her hand and smiled. "We should do this more often."

"Yes we should. I miss our time alone together."

Richard glanced over Leslie's shoulder at a print of Venice at carnival time, revealing dozens of carefree, merry faces. He felt like one of those faces. And why not? He was enjoying the company of his wife, feeling hopeful about Justin, and yes, after what had felt like an eternity of anguish, he could finally see an end in sight.

I promise I'll never deceive you again, sweetheart.

Early the following afternoon, Richard found Leslie downstairs looking sideways at a partially finished work of a three-dimensional flying chessboard with human pieces.

"What in the world is this?"

"How do you like my queens?"

"That one looks like Hillary Clinton."

"What about the other one?"

Richard screwed up his face. "Uh, I don't know, some pompous-looking bitch."

Leslie snickered. "Margaret Thatcher, you fool. What do you think?"

He laughed. "If you say so."

As Richard came back upstairs he wondered how he would produce a highlights-only edited version on DVD from the original, suitable for mailing. He ruled out using his laptop. Once you imprint the hard drive, the "evidence" could never be completely erased.

A solution finally came the next day during his afternoon clinic. He would transfer the footage from the DVD to his trusty old camcorder, and then transfer selected parts back to a blank DVD. Tedious but untraceable.

Richard pulled his car into the park and reached for his phone.

"Hi Cathy, how are you?"

"Just fine, Richard. How are things?"

"I got it."

"Got what?"

"The recording."

"Lundh?"

"And Angela, in his bedroom."

"Really! Wow. How the hell did you manage that?"

"Like they say, when there is a will, there is a way." Richard waited. "You still there?"

"Yeah. I'm just shocked, I guess."

"Me too. In his own bed, no less."

"No, I mean, that you actually did it."

"I know. I'm kind of shocked myself. My head is still spinning. Anyway, I was wondering, I need to edit the master using my camcorder and a DVD player, but I'd rather not do it at home. Would it be possible for me to come over to your place and do it there? We could watch it together while I do the edit."

"Watch the video? I don't know, Richard. It sounds kind of creepy."

"It's not going to be creepy. It'll be fine. I just have to get this done and over with, the sooner the better."

"I guess you haven't told Leslie, have you?"

"No, I . . . believe me, I wanted to, but . . ."

"Never mind. Does Friday night work for you?"

Later that evening, Richard approached Leslie in the basement.

"Sweetheart, would you mind terribly if I switched my tennis night to this Friday instead of tomorrow night?"

"Sure. No problem."

"The guy I'm playing has the flu. He says he'll probably be fine by then."

"Whatever. That's fine."

He turned away and silently cursed himself.

Could you look any guiltier?

Richard knocked on Cathy's door promptly at eight, briefcase in hand.

She looked at him, expressionless. "Come in."

She led him into the family room and disappeared into the kitchen. "Let's see, I have a Cabernet and a Pinot Noir."

"The Pinot is fine."

He hooked up his camcorder to her DVD player and inserted the disc. Cathy rested a glass of wine on a table next to him and sat on the couch.

Richard frowned. "Where's your glass?"

"I'm good. I had my quota for the day at supper."

He turned on the television and inserted an 8 mm tape into his camcorder. He aimed the remote at the DVD player, looked at Cathy, and pushed the button.

Lundh and Angela came into view on both the television and the tiny screen of the video camera.

"What can I get you to drink?"

"Gin and tonic is fine."

Cathy threw her hands up to her mouth. "Oh my God."

Richard raised his glass. "I'd like to dedicate this viewing to the sad memory of my poor endoscopy center, conceived by yours truly, Richard Chase, stolen from under my nose by that malicious bastard Jack Lundh." He brought the glass to his lips, breathed in deeply, and drank, nearly finishing the wine in a single gulp.

Cathy slipped into the kitchen and returned with the wine bottle and another glass. "I think I might need just a drop or two."

Richard poured himself more wine and took another large gulp. Lundh and Angela sat in the family room. The picture was crystal clear. The audio was slightly muffled but adequate. Angela did most of the talking, about her job, her mother, and a few other incidental things.

Richard shifted in his seat, drained his glass, and gave himself a generous refill. "Don't worry; it's coming."

"But why does she want a divorce?" the woman asked, stroking his thigh.

"Because I work too much, I don't like her crazy sisters, I'm too fat, I don't like to have a house full of people every weekend, I'm not happy about her swilling down a quart of wine every day."

Richard glanced at Cathy and groaned. "Jesus, are they never going to shut up?"

Cathy looked away.

Angela kissed Lundh. They got up and left the room. The screen went blank for a moment. The dimly lit bedroom suddenly appeared.

Richard jumped to his feet, listing briefly to one side, and poured himself his third glass of wine, finishing the bottle. "Holy shit, this is it!"

Cathy gulped down her half glass of wine. "Hey, calm down, will you?"

With conventional video, the dimly lit bedroom would not have been visible, but the infrared technology came to the rescue, producing a remarkably clear image of both Lundh and Angela in dark outline yet with distinctly recognizable features. The audio was also excellent, much better than in the family room.

Richard stared with disbelieving eyes at the scene unfolding before them. A tirade of scorn poured from his mouth. Every muffled whisper, every word, every vocalized pleasure, from their initial embrace to their climax, brought a new howl of derision. The couple fell back onto the bed. The picture went blank.

Richard hit the "off" button and shook his fist in the air. "Perfect!" He turned to look at Cathy, but she wasn't in her chair. "Hey, where did you go?

Cathy emerged from the kitchen carrying a tray with two large mugs of steaming coffee. "I think it's time to sober up."

"Did you see that? Did you see—?"

"I saw enough of it." She handed him a cup. "Here, get this down you, and don't spill it."

Richard ignored the coffee. "Cathy, what's wrong? Don't you see? I got him. I got the bastard by the balls!"

Cathy set the cup down on the coffee table and shook her head. "I don't know, Richard. It was okay before, when you first talked about it, but now . . ."

"But now *what*?"

Cathy's face tightened. "I don't know. It's hard to explain."

"You believe that poor victim shit? Is that what this is about?"

"No! Absolutely not. He's a cheating bastard. Believe me, nobody more than me wants his nuts in a meat grinder. It's just this whole video thing, it feels . . . *dirty*."

Richard stepped toward her on unsteady legs. "Dirty? You want to know what dirty is? What that malicious son of a bitch did to *me*!" He poked himself in the chest.

Cathy took his hand and squeezed it. "This is a mistake, Richard. A big mistake."

Richard felt a rush of heat into his face. "Really? What the hell do you know about it? Ever get your life's dream snatched away from under your nose? Just taken away for no reason? Ever been slapped in the face and pissed on in public, all because you stand for something worthwhile? Everything I worked for, *everything*, down the drain. You think this is easy? You think I enjoy breaking into houses, acting like a criminal? What the hell else was I supposed to do? I thought *you* understood."

Cathy lowered her head.

Richard pulled himself away from her. "Never mind, I'm wasting my breath."

He headed down the hall. "Where the hell is your bathroom?"

—ɱ—

Cathy flopped back on the couch. She heard the bathroom door slam and his stream hit the water. A moment later, she jumped up.

With lightning-fast hands, she snatched the 8 mm cassette from the camcorder, stuffed it in her pocket, replaced it with one of the blank cassettes in the open briefcase, and dove back into her recliner, her guts churning.

Richard returned a moment later, retrieved the DVD, picked up his camcorder and briefcase, and headed toward the door without looking at her.

"Richard, I don't want you to send that recording."

He turned toward her and stared, stone-faced, saying nothing.

"I mean it. Destroy it. It's all a catastrophic mistake."

He walked out, slamming the door behind him.

Cathy sat in stunned silence. She fell back onto the couch,

and pulled her knees tightly to her chest. Tears of anger, shame, and guilt streamed down her cheeks.

Why did I ever get involved?

She felt stained, deep inside the marrow of her bones.

She hated him.

Cathy glared at the 8 mm tape in her hand. What good would this thing do? She hadn't had the time or the guts to switch out the master DVD. When he found the blank tape in his camcorder, he was bound to suspect her of making the switch. She could only imagine the uncontrollable rage he would feel toward her.

Just destroy the damned thing.

She was about to toss the 8 mm tape into the garbage, and then stopped.

Maybe if she just saw that lying bastard again, she'd be okay with it.

She inserted the tape into her own video camera, found the discussion in the living room, and hit "play."

The voices on the tape took her breath away. Lundh and Angela—and *Richard*! To her astonishment, Richard's commentary during their viewing filled the room, as if he were still standing next to her. If anything, his voice was louder than Lundh's or Angela's, who sounded oddly distant.

Cathy sat back, shaking her head. A moment later, the real bombshell hit. Her own voice, stinging her like a slap in the face, could also be faintly heard. Aghast, she ran through the entire recording. Richard's malicious comments rang out like a bell. Fortunately, her own voice remained barely audible. Could she be identified? She played the recording again. Not a chance. She breathed a sigh of relief.

She dropped the video camera onto the couch as if it were poison, staggered into the bedroom, and collapsed onto the bed.

23

Cathy peered out her bedroom window. The wind howled. A steady rain fell from blotches of gray and black clouds. She thought of the horrible events of the night before. How in the world could their voices have become superimposed on the recording? While staring at her breakfast, she remembered having had some repairs done at a small electronics shop in town about a year ago. Time for a visit.

The tiny store was cluttered with merchandise and boxes lying on the floor and lining the walls, leaving barely enough room to enter. Cathy explained her mystery to an elderly gentleman behind the counter, who bore a striking resemblance to Abraham Lincoln. The old man's brow furrowed. He blew his nose with a yellow-stained handkerchief, coughed up an enormous amount of phlegm, and swallowed. She turned away.

A much younger Abe Lincoln appeared from the back of the store with a small microwave in his arms.

"Thanks, Dad, I'll take it from here."

He listened to Cathy's story and smiled. "I know exactly what happened. He messed up the connection between the DVD recorder and the camcorder."

"I don't understand. How can screwing up the connection give you *more* information?"

"It's easy. I'll bet you his camcorder is an older model that has a separate plug-in site for audio and video. He plugged in the video part first, but then either forgot to plug in the audio part, or didn't make sure it was in tight."

"I still don't get it. How did that cause our voices to be recorded?"

Young Abe laughed. "Let me guess. You were watching the DVD on the TV while you were recording with the camcorder, right?"

"Right."

"When the plug is not inserted tightly, the little microphone on the camcorder stays on and records the audio in the room, which in your case was both the audio from the TV *and* your conversation while you watched it."

Cathy insisted young Abe take twenty dollars for his time. Discovering the blunder was great, but Richard still had the master DVD and clearly had every intention of using it. Thank God he didn't have a copy with their voices superimposed on it.

He had to be stopped. But how?

Richard poured a fresh cup of coffee. The terrible scene from the previous night replayed itself in his achy head. How could he have been so awful to her, drinking too much and shooting off his mouth? If only he had begged for understanding, perhaps he could have won her over. Instead, he had driven his only ally away.

The house was quiet. Justin was sleeping and Leslie was out visiting a neighbor. Time to create an edited DVD. Richard hit "play" on his camcorder. The small screen lit up blue. He impatiently hit "rewind." To his surprise, the tape stopped in less than a second. He advanced the tape several seconds and hit "play"—more blue. He ran through the entire tape—nothing but blue. He checked all his other 8 mm tapes and found they were all blank. He taped a few minutes of his master DVD onto one of the blank tapes. The camcorder viewing screen sprang to life with Lundh and Angela. What the hell had happened? Probably some connection screwup, he figured. All that for nothing, he thought, shaking his head.

Richard gathered up the 8 mm tapes and threw them into his desk drawer. Wait a minute. How many of those little tapes did he have? He threw open the drawer and tossed five tapes on the desk. Didn't he initially have six? He certainly hadn't misplaced the copied tape. He distinctly remembered putting it into his open briefcase. He retraced his steps. He caught his breath.

No way, she wouldn't have.

If her intent had been to stop him, surely she would have snatched *both* the DVD and the 8 mm tape. The whole thing made no sense. Her DVD player must have screwed up. He probably just misplaced a blank tape.

Richard called the neighbor. Leslie wouldn't be back for about another hour. He got to work. In no time, he had four DVD copies of the bedroom scene. He inserted a DVD and brief note in each of three bubble-padded manila envelopes, addressed to Boutique Coco, Lundh's office, and Lundh's home. He affixed correct postage and sealed the packages. He locked them in his briefcase, removed his latex gloves, and placed the briefcase in his car trunk.

As he slammed the trunk closed, Cathy's fiery words flashed across his mind: *This is a mistake, Richard. A big mistake . . . I don't want you to send that recording . . . Destroy it. It's all a catastrophic mistake.*

His back stiffened.

That evening after dinner, Richard went out to get some gas and called Cathy.

"What do you want?" she asked.

Her abruptness sent a chill down his spine.

"I just called to say how very sorry I am for the crazy things I said and the terrible way I acted last night. I was an insensitive pig. I'm sorry I treated you so badly. The red wine didn't help. I can't drink much of that stuff, but that's no excuse."

"I hadn't noticed."

"Look, it really kills me to do this, but I want to let you know I've decided to not send the recording. I hate the bastard, but I guess it's just too nasty a thing to do, even to him. It's not going to help me anyway. I'm just going to destroy the recording. I'm sorry. I really screwed up. I hope you can forgive me."

He waited. "Are you there?"

"I'm here. I'm just a little surprised, that's all. Do you really mean this?"

"Yes, I do. I let my anger lead me down the wrong path. Fortunately, it's not too late to do the right thing."

"You're right, Richard, it's not too late. I'm glad you've come to your senses. I accept your apology."

"Thank you. That means a lot to me. Well, I'll talk to you soon. Good night."

Moments later, Richard found himself before a mailbox at the end of a strip mall. His right hand tightly clutched his bombshell packages while his left hand firmly squeezed the mailbox handle. He couldn't remember a single thing between the time he had ended his call with Cathy and now. How had he even gotten here?

My God, I could have killed somebody on the road. What's happening to me?

He released the handle and stepped back. Cold sweat flashed over his face. A wave of nausea came over him.

He opened the mail slot, slammed it shut, reopened it, and thrust his trembling, gloved hand inside. Humiliation, indignation, and condemnation burned his insides like chlorine gas. Leslie and Cathy flashed across his mind. His heart pounded.

Drop them, dammit, drop them.

With every muscle in his body tight as a drum, with all the strength and will he could muster, he tried to release his grip.

His fingers held on tight.

At that moment, standing rigid as a post, one arm in the mailbox, oblivious to the world around him, the realization hit him like a thunderbolt. He couldn't do it. No matter how deep the injury to him, his loss, his pain, he just couldn't do it.

He yanked his hand out of the mailbox. On the way out, the DVDs struck the inside wall of the box, slipped from his grasp like a wet bar of soap, and fell in.

He froze, panic-stricken. A moment later, his legs turned to mush. He slumped to the sidewalk, his sweaty palms sliding along the cool blue box as if trying to hold himself up.

Oh God, what have I done?

Richard spent Sunday at home with Leslie and Justin, reading the paper, pulling weeds, removing a few dead limbs from his trees, and cleaning out the already-clean shed in the backyard—anything to avoid the uneasiness swirling in his mind.

In the afternoon, he and Justin rearranged a few storage items in the basement. Things were looking up between them. Justin agreed to join his dad for a Red Sox game the following weekend.

On Monday morning, following his teaching rounds, Richard pitched the surveillance equipment at the city dump. He had initially planned on retrieving the bugs from Lundh's house, but couldn't bring himself to perform yet another break-in. No matter. When or if they were eventually discovered, the equipment couldn't possibly be traced back to him.

On Tuesday, he awoke at dawn. He struggled through his morning appointments, unable to concentrate. Patients spoke, but the only voices he could hear were those of Leslie, McAllister, Starkey, and Cathy. He tried to focus on the faces of his patients, but he kept envisioning Lundh ripping open the package, discovering the DVD, and reading the note.

The mail arrived just before noon, landing on Richard's

desk with a thump. He turned his head away. Lundh's first case of the day was a bowel resection at two o'clock. Would the poor bastard check his mail before his case? For the patient's sake, he hoped not.

At four thirty, Richard went into the surgeon's change room. Lundh's locker door was partially open. He looked inside—empty. Had Lundh still not shown up for his case? He wandered into the hallway bridging the post-op recovery area and the operating rooms. Perhaps he could casually ask one of the OR nurses about how the afternoon was going.

Lundh suddenly burst through the automatic doors to the endoscopy/surgery suite, strands of salt-and-pepper hair dangling over his glistening forehead, his white coat flying in the breeze behind him. Richard hid behind the nursing station. He caught a glimpse of the envelope tucked under his arm.

Richard retreated to the closest stairwell, collapsed onto a gray, cement step, and buried his face in his hands. Night after night, he had imagined celebrating this moment, this spectacular accomplishment of righteous vengeance. Instead, here he was, sitting in a dusty stairwell with his head in his hands. He squeezed his eyes shut. Where was this joy of victory he had so eagerly anticipated?

Jack Lundh peered out his front window, straining to identify the passing cars. He glanced at the wall clock and took another sip of coffee. Jeremy S. Lloyd, private detective and retired Boston police lieutenant, was fifteen minutes late for his return visit.

From the moment Jack had opened that envelope two weeks ago, he had been driven by a burning obsession to punish his wife. To consider anyone else seemed absurd, despite her vehement denial. They were, after all, enduring a loveless marriage, and he was having an affair. As careful as he had been, Sharon had probably stumbled upon his infidelity and become hell-bent on revenge. She could easily have hired someone to set it all up while he was at work or away on a conference.

He cast his mind back to Lloyd's comment: "Been doing this a long time . . . usually ends up being the spouse."

Finally, a car pulled into his driveway. Jack ushered Lloyd into the kitchen and suffered through some small talk, waiting for the news.

Lloyd opened his briefcase. "Anything exciting at the Lundh residence since we last spoke?"

Jack looked away. "I've been told my marital status will soon be changing. She's living over at her sister's in Cambridge."

"She didn't kick you out?"

"I offered to leave."

"Anything else?"

"I asked her again if she did it."

"And?"

"She told me to fuck off. She's still accusing me of making the video. So what have you found? Talk to me."

Lloyd pulled out a notebook and cleared his throat. "I was able to pick up fourteen calls to five different people. She said she got the video in the mail and had no idea what it was. She watched it and was flabbergasted."

"Flabbergasted?"

"That's the word she used. She said it must have been your own personal home video that slipped into enemy hands. She gave the same story to everybody."

Jack hit the table with his fist. "Beautiful! She sets me up then makes me look like a schmuck to all her friends. She's got to be lying!"

"Take it easy. Did you search the house and her e-mail?"

"With a fine tooth comb. Nothing. What about the GPS?"

Lloyd shook his head. "I followed her home from work for five straight days and on three occasions when she went out at night. Nothing. She always went directly home from work. On the nights she went out, it was for groceries or shopping at the mall. I was hoping she'd lead me to somebody who might have helped her with the bugging, but no such luck. In fact, I never saw her with anyone but her sister."

"What about the equipment?"

"Fancy stuff. I plan to check with all the mail services for delivery of surveillance equipment. I drew up a list of companies that make the stuff, mostly overseas. I also need to talk to one of your neighbors. I'm hoping they saw something."

Jack rose from the kitchen table and looked out the window over the sink. "It's *got* to be her."

"Listen, Jack, it could still be Sharon. Hell, it probably is, but I'm afraid we also need to start looking elsewhere. I want you to think—is there anybody else, *anybody*, we need to consider? Everybody has enemies."

"Enemies?" He stiffened and looked away. "No, of course not."

"Well, think about it some more, okay? I'll give you a call in about a week, after I've tidied up a few loose ends. If you think of anything, call me. I'll let myself out."

Jack stretched out on the couch in the family room. He turned on a movie, but couldn't concentrate.

A week later, Lloyd called.

"I checked all the local post office branches and a bunch of surveillance companies. Zilch. I showed the DVD to a surveillance expert. He agrees it must have been a professional job using top-notch equipment, but he couldn't be more specific. Let's see, I also spoke to your neighbor and the security guards at the gate. Nobody saw anything suspicious."

"Is that it?"

"I'm afraid so, Jack. I've hit a wall on this one."

"Jesus, Lloyd, what am I supposed to do now?"

"I wish I knew. You can have another PI look at it. I doubt that's going to help, but it might make you feel better. Maybe you need to just leave it alone for a little while. In the meantime, if I think of anything, I'll let you know. Keep in touch."

That night, Jack tossed and turned until the sun came up. He reviewed it all in his mind and resolved to take Lloyd's advice. He would lie low for a while and try to work through his anger and frustration. At this point, he had no other choice.

Cathy sat at her kitchen table, her head in her hands, staring at a cup of cold coffee. She tried to convince herself her foul mood was hormonal, but she knew better. The truth was, after almost four weeks, despite the apology, she still couldn't completely shake off the emotional pain Richard had inflicted on her that horrible evening. She had promised herself to blot his drunk, angry ass out of her life forever and to move on. But that nightmarish evening kept replaying in her mind. Why couldn't she let go of this?

Had yet another man betrayed her? She had to know, for certain, *now*.

Cathy reached for the phone book on the kitchen counter, blocked her Caller ID, and placed a call.

"Boutique Coco, can I help you?"

"Can I, uh, speak to Sharon Lundh?"

"Speaking."

"Mrs. Lundh, I'm afraid I can't tell you who I am, but—"

"What's this about? Who are you?"

Cathy took a deep breath. "Please tell me if the following words have a special meaning to you: sex video."

The line remained silent.

"Please, Sharon, if your answer is yes, I have important information for you, information that will *help* you."

"Yes."

Cathy caught her breath. "I need to know for sure. What was she wearing around her neck?"

"A scarf. An ugly scarf! Now who are you? What can you tell me?"

She cut off the call. Angry tears flew down her cheeks.

—⚊⚊—

A half hour later, Cathy's doorbell rang. Before she could move off the couch, Zoe burst in.

"Cat, are you okay? I got here as quick as I could."

Cathy met her best friend with a forced smile and a tight hug. "Thanks for coming over so quick. What did you do, fly over here?"

"Just about. What's going on? The sound of your voice . . . frightened me."

They sat on the couch in the family room in front of the fireplace. Two glasses of wine sat on the coffee table in front of them. Cathy picked up the glasses and handed one to Zoe. "Drink up, Z. You're going to need it."

"Jesus, you're freaking me out. You don't have cancer or something, do you?"

Cathy took a large sip of wine and tried to smile. "No Z, I don't have cancer. I'm just so angry, I could scream."

Cathy recounted the entire story; from the time Richard Chase first contacted her to her shocking discovery that Chase had sent the DVD to Lundh. When she was through, she gulped down the last of her glass of Pinot and looked at Zoe.

Zoe raised her eyebrows. "Wow. You sure you aren't making this up?"

"I wish I were," Cathy said quietly.

Zoe shifted on the couch toward Cathy. "I'm sorry, Cat. I can only imagine what you must be feeling."

Cathy looked directly into the eyes of her best friend, the person she had shared so many secrets with over the years. She hesitated, not sure what to say, what to ask for, or even what to think. She stared at her empty wine glass.

"I don't know what to do, Z. I don't know whether to just walk away, rip a strip off his ass, or choke him out."

"Well, if you'd like my advice—"

Cathy thrust herself up on the edge of the couch, bumping Zoe's knee. "I don't even care that much about the damned DVD. I just can't stand being lied to. Again! By yet another man who I liked, even admired! I'm sick of it! Sick to death!"

Zoe gently pushed her back. "Take it easy, Cat. Listen to me. Wash your hands of the whole disgusting mess. Stay away from Chase and forget it ever happened."

Cathy sighed and lowered her head. She felt her body go limp. "I knew you'd say that."

"Of course you knew I'd say that, because it's the only sensible thing to do, and you know it."

Tears suddenly filled Cathy's eyes. "I . . . I don't think I can do that, Z."

Zoe grabbed a box of tissues from the table and handed it to Cathy. "Why not? Come on girl, you can't let this shit eat you alive."

Cathy turned toward her friend. "I know that. I know I should just walk away, like I *always* just walk away when I'm abused. But it just doesn't feel . . . *enough*. It isn't *closure*, you know what I mean?"

"So what's your idea of closure? Stabbing him in the chest?"

"I just want to, I don't know, teach him a *lesson*. A good, hard lesson. That's all."

"A lesson? Oh, so now you're the schoolteacher teaching the naughty boy a lesson, or maybe all the naughty boys in the world a lesson? Is that what this is about? Come on, Cat, what is that going to accomplish?"

Cathy shrugged.

"And how do you propose to get this satisfaction?"

Cathy looked into the fireplace. "I don't know."

"Why don't you just call the cops?"

"Are you nuts? Have you forgotten I'm an accomplice? I said I'm angry, not crazy."

Zoe smiled. "Not sure about that actually, the crazy part I mean." She finished the last of her wine and refilled their glasses. "Have you eaten today?"

Zoe found some cheese and crackers and brought them back to the family room. She lifted a slice of cheese to her mouth and stopped. "Here's an idea. Why not just anonymously send the DVD to Lundh?"

Cathy frowned. "What? Why would I do that? He's already got it."

Zoe smiled. "Yeah, but not the *overdubbed* version. Didn't you say Chase identified himself? Actually said his name?"

Cathy gasped. She opened her mouth to speak, but hesitated. "No. No, I couldn't do that. That would be—"

"You want to teach him a lesson? Let the real victim do your dirty work for you. At the same time, you'd be helping out Lundh."

"Helping out Lundh?" The thought tightened her belly. "I don't think so, Z."

"Why not? I thought you felt bad for him, about what happened."

"I wouldn't go that far. I mean, I wouldn't exactly put it that way. Sure, I wish he hadn't sent the DVD, but not because I like the guy or feel bad for him. I think he's a bastard. I didn't want him to send it because the surveillance was just plain wrong, period. It doesn't matter what I think about Lundh. Unfortunately, that didn't hit me until I actually saw the video. I don't know, maybe it was just a game before then. Anyway, this isn't about Jack Lundh. At this point, I really don't give a shit about how any of this affects him, one way or the other."

"Okay, fine. Who cares about Lundh? But you gotta admit, if you can't just walk away, if you must pull the trigger, that's a bullet that would do some damage. It might also help to get some of that blood off your hands, if you know what I mean."

Cathy straightened her back and looked at Zoe.

Zoe rested her hand on Cathy's shoulder. "Hey, don't get me wrong, Cat. I'm not saying you should do that. I still think the best thing is to just forget about the whole damned thing."

Cathy took a deep breath. "I don't know. I think I'm more confused than ever."

Zoe smiled. "What are friends for? Look, why don't you just sleep on it? It's amazing how just a little time can give you a totally different outlook. Look at you. You're pissed off enough to bite the ass end out of a skunk. That's no time to make any decisions. Anyway, like I said, if you want my advice, just forget the whole sordid mess and move on."

Zoe gave Cathy a hug. "Are you okay?"

Cathy nodded without emotion. "I'm fine."

"All right, I'll call you tomorrow. Get some sleep."

Zoe took a few steps toward the foyer, stopped, and turned toward Cathy. "Can I ask you just one question?"

Cathy rubbed her cheeks. "Sure."

"I meant to ask you before, but it slipped my mind. It's bugging me a little. Why did you do it? I mean, why did you get involved with this crazy scheme in the first place?"

Cathy sighed and shook her head. "I wish I hadn't."

"It just seems really odd that you would allow yourself to get involved in that kind of thing. It's kind of like jumping into a shark tank, you know?"

Cathy looked at Zoe, hoping she would drop it, but she knew her friend well enough to know that she would have to come clean. She opened her mouth to speak, but couldn't find the words. "I don't know, Zoe, I—"

"Zoe? You haven't called me that since the last time I pissed you off. I do believe I've hit a nerve."

"You haven't hit a nerve!"

"Was there more to your friendship than you're admitting? You know, were you—?"

"Don't be ridiculous. He's married."

"I didn't ask you if he were married."

Cathy felt a rush of heat into her face. "Look, I considered him a close friend. He had helped me get through my breakup with no strings attached. I liked him a lot, personally and professionally. What the hell's wrong with that? So when he told me how he got screwed by this asshole, I just . . ."

"You just saw a chance to grind another cheating bastard into the ground. Is that it?"

"You're damned right that's it!" She lowered her head. "I just didn't realize . . ." she said, barely above a whisper, wiping away a new wave of tears.

Zoe gave Cathy a hug. "It's okay. I'm sorry. I didn't mean to upset you. I just want to make sure that you're being honest with yourself about how you got into this mess. Otherwise, you're not going to get out of it the right way."

Cathy smiled. "I don't know what I'd do without you."

"You going to be okay tonight?"

"I'll be fine. Thanks for coming over."

Cathy dragged herself up to her bedroom, took a sleeping pill, and flopped into bed, hoping for a long, deep sleep. Three hours later, having not yet closed her eyes, she threw back the covers. As if sleepwalking, she found herself in the family room with her finger on the "play" button.

Without knowing why, or even wanting to do so, she watched the video. Again.

She felt heat and rage and anger. Suddenly, everything became clear. She knew what she had to do. To her amazement, in the blink of an eye, the weight of the world vanished. She felt light, calm, even peaceful.

She closed her eyes and fell asleep.

28

As days turned into weeks, Richard's preoccupation with the "Lundh affair" gradually waned. The whole incredible incident was beginning to feel more like an absurd dream. The time had come to concentrate on the present. He had a loving wife. He was making progress with his son, and he still had a thriving practice.

Richard couldn't, however, completely suppress a lingering uneasiness. Had Lundh initiated an investigation? If so, surely the name "Chase" had surfaced at some point. Yet seven weeks had passed, and he still hadn't been contacted. Perhaps in his shame, Lundh had decided not to pursue it.

Richard stepped out of the shower and stood naked before the full-length bathroom mirror. Time to get his game face on for the hospital's annual tennis tournament held at his club this weekend. He had won the previous two years and had been looking forward to defending his title. Sixteen players were enrolled in a sudden death, best-of-three-sets format. The first round would be played this evening at eight o'clock, followed by the next two games on Saturday. The finalists would play for the championship on Sunday afternoon at three.

Richard beat his first two opponents in straight sets, but he found his game below his usual standard. In the third match on Saturday, he played poorly, but his overweight opponent fatigued, giving Richard the win. At four o'clock, he dragged his weary body home.

He awoke on Sunday morning achy and exhausted. Leslie suggested the three of them head over to the club for brunch. If he wished, Richard could stretch out and relax in the back seat of the SUV on the way over. Justin agreed to join them for a quick bite before meeting some friends at the pool.

Richard was hungry, but the grilled turkey breast sandwich turned his stomach. He forced down a small salad and picked at a few fries.

Thirty minutes before the championship match, he went to the court. The stands were empty, except for a young Asian woman with a baby. The referee and two line judges shared a joke at the net with a tall Asian man bouncing a tennis ball. The man, probably in his mid-twenties, had straight, shoulder-length, jet-black hair parted in the middle, held in place with a sweatband. He wore an oversized, white tennis shirt that hung over long, baggy, black tennis shorts. Richard had heard that T. N. Lee, a Korean recently hired in the financial aid office, was an excellent player.

Richard approached Lee and extended his hand. "Richard Chase. I hear you're quite a player."

Lee smiled. "I've been told you're not so bad yourself."

A few minutes before the match, Richard glanced toward the stands. There was Lundh, sitting in the third row, right behind Leslie and Justin. Leslie waved and smiled. Richard pretended not to see her.

The match was a disaster from the outset. Lee's serves and volleys flew over the net like bullets. Richard lost the first set six to two, gasping for breath.

Before the second set, he stole a glance into the stands. To his surprise, he spotted Cathy, sitting alone in the back row, tucked away in a corner. Strange to see her here, he thought. She had never come to any of the other hospital tournaments.

Richard's next serve hit the frame of his racket and bounced over the stands into the adjacent court. The gallery buzzed. He checked the strings with nervous fingers.

The match finally came to a merciful end with Richard losing in straight sets. He hobbled to the net, exhausted, sore, and a little embarrassed.

"Well done, Lee. I never had a chance."

"Thanks."

Richard went to the sideline opposite the stands to retrieve his sports bag, vowing to make this his last year in the tournament. From out of the corner of his eye, he saw Cathy, followed by Leslie, crossing the court toward him.

"Hey, Richard. Long time no see."

Richard looked up and forced a smile. She wore a conspicuously revealing pink summer dress, a strong perfume, and suggestive eyes.

Leslie came up behind her, hands on her hips, frowning. Cathy stepped forward and laid her hand on Richard's shoulder.

"Don't feel bad about the game, *dear*. He's young enough to be your son."

Richard's eyes darted between the two women.

"Uh, Cathy, have you met my wife, Leslie?"

Leslie forcefully cleared her throat. "She introduced herself before the game."

Richard glanced at both women. "Surprised to see you here, Cathy," he said casually, his insides tightening.

Cathy chuckled. "Don't be silly, *dear*. You promised to be in the finals and win again. I'm shocked to see you let me down. I didn't think that was possible from you."

Leslie stormed off the court. Richard's insides convulsed. He glared at Cathy and chased his wife into the main lobby.

"Leslie, hang on. Where are you going?"

Leslie stopped abruptly and spun around. "Just tell me, how long have you been fucking her?"

"Oh my God. I never . . . Come with me. Please. I need to tell you something about this woman."

She glared at him.

"Les, please give me the chance to explain."

She stood rigid and silent.

"Come on, Les. Please—"

She threw her hands in the air. "Okay, all right! Start talking."

He led her to a patio table next to the abandoned outdoor pool. His mind raced frantically for some kind of plausible explanation.

Oh God, should I tell her about the surveillance? No, don't you dare. Anything but that.

"She divorced an abusive husband a year ago. She was a mess. Since the divorce, I've been giving her advice and encouragement. Emotional support. Call it what you will. The problem is, nothing seemed to help. A couple of months ago, out of nowhere, she made a pass at me in the doctor's parking lot." The lie tightened his insides. "She suggested we get together. I was shocked. I told her, maybe not in the nicest way, I wasn't interested. I was kind of hard on her, actually. She got pissed off and left. I haven't called her since."

"You've been *calling* her?"

"Before the parking lot incident, yes, on occasion. Mostly, she would call me. Anyway, like I said, I put a stop to it, in no uncertain terms. That little act you saw . . . I guess she's just trying to—"

"You never had sex with her?"

"Never! I never wanted to, and I never would have. I just wanted to help her."

"Why didn't you ever tell me this?"

"I didn't want to upset you, get you thinking the wrong things, like now."

Leslie shook her head. "I don't know."

"Look, if we were having an affair, the last thing she'd do is advertise it to you."

Her face softened. "I'm sorry. I guess I overreacted."

Richard rose and hugged her. "No, sweetheart, I'm sorry, for all of this. Forgive me?"

"Don't I always?"

Richard looked away.

Leslie sighed and shook her head. "I'm going to run a few errands before the awards banquet. I'll be back soon."

Richard watched her disappear into the parking lot. He crossed his arms and shut his eyes. A gust of wind rippled some remaining water at the bottom of the pool. Why in the world had Cathy done this? Could she still be bitter over their last get-together? She had seemed okay when he had called her. Could she have found out? No. Impossible.

Or was it?

No way. Forget it.

He thought of this latest obscene lie to Leslie,

manufactured on the spot, and cringed. Enough was enough. He would tell his wife everything and throw himself on her mercy. Tonight, when they got home, he would finally find the courage to come clean. He owed this to her. She deserved so much better.

About an hour later, Richard stepped out of the locker room shower, still stiff and sore, but feeling a little better.

"Richard? Is Richard Chase here?"

Richard froze.

"Hello? Is Richard—"

"I'm in here." He could barely get the words out.

Jack Lundh appeared from behind a row of lockers. He grinned. "I'm glad I caught you. I want to make sure you're going to be at the awards ceremony."

Richard awkwardly adjusted his towel around his waist. "I'll be there."

"Hey, nice try out there. Lee's a great player."

"Yeah."

"See you at the dinner?"

"Yeah."

Richard dropped into a chair next to his locker, his heart pounding in his chest.

What the hell was that all about?

At seven, Leslie and Richard strolled into the crowded banquet hall. Justin had elected to forgo the awards ceremony in favor of the weight room and tennis courts. Richard immediately scanned the room for Cathy. To his great relief, he didn't see her.

He spotted Lundh and Andrew Steckle, the hospital's CEO, talking near the podium. Next to them, trophies and gifts sat on a table. Richard and Leslie sat at a table close to the podium with three other couples.

Richard kept his head down and said little during the meal, unable to clear his mind of Cathy and the unsettling notion of having to accept his prize from Lundh. He didn't touch his Merlot.

Steckle stepped up to the microphone. "Ladies and gentlemen, thank you for helping to make the Fifth Annual Boston Civic Hospital Tennis Tournament and awards banquet a terrific success. We welcome you and hope you enjoy yourselves this evening. I'd like to thank all the participants in the tournament, especially Dr. Jack Lundh, our tournament organizer, and, of course, our finalists, Mr. T. N. Lee and Dr. Richard Chase."

Polite applause filled the room.

Steckle called the two finalists to come up. Richard took his place next to Lee.

"And now, I would like to call up Dr. Jack Lundh for the presentations."

Richard tightened his jaw.

Lundh greeted Richard with a warm smile and a brisk handshake.

"If you don't mind my saying, Richard, it was a case of the old and the young, with the young prevailing."

Richard accepted his second-place trophy and small, gift-wrapped prize with an awkward smile and a quiet "thank you" amid a smattering of applause. He stuffed the prize into his jacket pocket.

Lundh wrapped his arm around Richard's shoulder, widened his smile, and, as if sharing a joke with a good friend in private, whispered into his ear, "It's over, motherfucker."

A jolt of electricity ripped through Richard. He barely made it back to his seat, soaking in sweat.

Leslie reached for his arm. "Richard, honey, what's wrong?

Richard recoiled, bumping the table with his elbow, knocking over a glass of red wine, sending it crashing onto the wooden floor. Wine splashed onto the cream-colored blouse and skirt of a woman seated next to Leslie. He blurted out an apology and bent over to pick up the shattered glass. The gift slipped out of his pocket and fell to the floor. The flimsy wrapping sprang open upon impact, partially exposing a DVD and a small piece of white paper. Richard snatched up the DVD and paper and disappeared without saying a word. He ran straight to the entertainment room next to the men's lockers, found it unoccupied, slammed the door shut, and jammed the disc into a DVD player. He held his breath as he hit "play."

The bedroom scene appeared with Richard's superimposed, scathing condemnation. The discovery hit him like a massive heart attack. He imagined Lundh watching the DVD and groaned. Every muscle in his body tightened. Panic flooded through him.

He grabbed the piece of paper in his pocket.

"I thought you might enjoy this fascinating mini docudrama. I call it *Unhinged*. Pity I can't personally thank the anonymous donor who sent it my way. If you get the chance, pass on my appreciation, will you? By the way, don't leave town anytime soon."

Richard ripped the paper to shreds, and then ejected the disc. With a guttural cry, he snapped it in half, and slammed it into the garbage can.

Bolting from the building, he raced up and down the rows of vehicles in a blind frenzy. He cracked his shin on a trailer hitch and howled in pain. He finally came upon Leslie's SUV. He fumbled with his keys, thrust the door open, and threw himself inside as if he were escaping gunfire. He threw the engine into reverse and hit the gas.

Get away, get away, just get away.

A dull thud came from the direction of his back bumper. Richard stomped on his brakes. A woman screamed. He threw open his door and scrambled to the rear of his SUV. A little girl, who looked to be no older than ten or eleven, lay sprawled on the pavement, her head partly hidden by his bumper and driver's side back wheel. The horrific image nearly paralyzed him. He buckled to his knees.

An onlooker ran toward them and cried, "Don't touch her! Don't move her head! Call 911! Call an ambulance!"

Leslie and Justin burst through the gathering crowd. Leslie began to cry hysterically. Justin stood mute, and then put his arm around his mother's shoulders. The police arrived two minutes later, followed by the paramedics and an ambulance. The child lay motionless with blood dripping from her right ear onto a tiny earring and strands of baby-fine blond hair.

Paramedics stabilized the little girl's neck with a collar and placed her in the ambulance. Police ushered the grief-stricken mother into their squad car. A large crowd had gathered around the scene. More police and another ambulance arrived. An officer kneeled over Richard.

"Sir, are you okay? What's your name? Can you tell me what happened?"

Richard stared at the spot where the little girl had been struck, his body shaking, tears racing down his cheeks.

The junior officer attempted a field sobriety test, but Richard didn't respond. The paramedics placed him on a stretcher and wheeled him to an ambulance.

Thirty minutes later, the police and most of the crowd had disappeared, but two people remained. Cathy stood close to the terrible spot, still as a mannequin, quietly sobbing, tears rolling down her face. Jack Lundh, drenched in sweat, stood several feet behind her, his disbelieving eyes fixed on the point of impact.

A call from the precinct regarding the child's status interrupted the eerie quiet of the squad car carrying Leslie and Justin to the station. Leslie gasped. The child, Amber Miller, had been rushed into emergency surgery for massive head trauma. Her young heart had stopped beating before the surgeon could intervene.

She was pronounced dead on the operating room table, three days before her tenth birthday.

29

Later that evening, Leslie and Justin sat opposite each other at their kitchen table. Leslie sipped on a strong rum and Coke, her second. Justin fidgeted with a saltshaker, looking out the window over the sink into the darkness.

Leslie emptied her glass with one final gulp and rubbed her eyes, unable to shake the horrific image of the little girl lying on the pavement behind the car. "Oh, God."

Justin turned toward her. "God has nothing to do with it. God didn't run over a ten-year-old girl."

Leslie jumped up. "Just what are you trying to say? It was a fucking accident!"

"Was he drinking?"

"He didn't have a single drop."

She sank back into her chair and looked down into her lap. "Justin, why do you hate your father?"

Justin lowered his head. "I never said I hated him."

"When he needs us most . . ." Leslie stood over her son. "Why, Justin, why the anger?"

Justin got up, kissed his mother on the cheek, and left the kitchen.

———∾∾∾———

Leslie lay in bed wide-awake. Images of the dying child's

body, her grief-stricken mother, and Richard sprawled out in the emergency-room bed, heavily sedated, unaware of the inevitable shock that would soon rip him to pieces, haunted her. He had looked terrible, half dead. Tears ran down her cheeks.

She replayed the instant when Richard had returned to the table after receiving his prize. She had never seen such fear in his face. Could his panic have had something to do with that disc? He had certainly seemed eager to hide it. Hopefully, he would be able to tell her something tomorrow.

The doorbell rang, causing her to flinch. The clock on her nightstand showed ten fifteen. She threw on a pair of jeans and sweater. Justin appeared at the top of the steps.

"Mom, who is it?"

Leslie peered through the peephole. There stood Lundh, glassy-eyed, rubbing his face. She clenched her fists and set her jaw.

"It's okay, Son," she said, loud enough for Lundh to hear. "It's just a colleague of Dad's."

She opened the door and glared at Lundh's haggard, motionless figure. "What do you want?"

"Leslie, can I talk to you?"

"You've got some nerve coming around here, you bastard."

Lundh dropped his gaze to the small space between them. "Please, if I could just have a moment."

They sat in the kitchen. Leslie leaned forward and fixed her eyes on him, as if she were about to pull a trigger. "What did you say to him at the ceremony?"

Lundh looked away. "How is he?" he asked softly.

"Why should you care? After what you did to him? How do you look at yourself in the mirror, you worthless piece of shit! And now this? I saw the terror on his face. You said something to him. Tell me now or so help me God . . ."

Lundh turned toward her and frowned. "Wait a minute. You don't know, I mean, what he did to me?"

"Of course I know. I know the whole story. He was just doing his job—" Leslie froze. The hair on the back of her neck came up. "What do you mean, what he did to you? What are you talking about?"

"You don't know about the . . . bugging?"

The word hit Leslie like a shovel on the back of her head. She looked at him, dumbfounded. "Bugging?" she asked, her voice barely audible.

Lundh fell back in his chair and groaned. "Oh God. For some reason, I don't know why, I assumed you knew. He had my house bugged, Leslie. I'm not proud of this, but I'm going to be honest. It's going to get out anyway. He caught me in bed with another woman. He sent the DVD to my wife and me. You didn't know that?"

Leslie rose from her chair and looked at him in disbelief. "He bugged your house?"

"Somebody, I don't know who, sent me the DVD. It's the strangest thing. You can hear his voice on it, clear as day, and another barely audible voice, I don't know who. He actually says his name on the recording, if you can believe it. Well, I was shocked. I flew into such a rage. I didn't know what to do. I called an attorney. Today, at the awards banquet, I gave him a copy of that DVD. I wanted to hurt him, Leslie, but as God is my witness . . ."

Lundh covered his face in his hands for a moment. "I wish this whole thing had never happened. After that hospital committee thing, I wish I had just gone out and got drunk and punched a wall and realized that that's how it goes and got it out of my system. But I didn't do that, did I? So the anger just grew inside me."

Within seconds, deep furrows filled his forehead and surrounded his eyes and mouth, aging him a decade. "Leslie, I know it's no excuse, but—"

"I don't want to hear any of this."

"Please! I've never said this to anybody. I *need* to say this. I *know* it's no excuse, I know that, but back in those committee meetings, I felt like I was being stomped on like an insect, in front of everybody. I felt belittled, embarrassed, treated like a bumbling fool. I didn't sleep for weeks. My practice suffered. If that wasn't bad enough, losing McAllister as a patient, the way it happened, in front of everybody—nurses, doctors, patients—I just lost my head."

"Get out of my house."

Lundh stood up. "I just wanted you to know, about the accident . . . I'm so sorry. I wish with all my heart I hadn't given him that DVD."

"But you're just fine calling a lawyer," Leslie said without emotion.

Lundh lowered his head and sighed. "Believe me, Leslie, this isn't easy for me. I feel terrible about what's happened today, but this bugging . . . I'm sorry, I just can't let it go."

"Please leave now."

Leslie watched Lundh shuffle down the stone path and drive off. She stood next to a window in the family room, unable to move, as if locked in some catatonic state of confusion and grief. Several minutes later, long after the lights of his vehicle vanished, she burst into a muffled cry.

30

The nurse gently tapped Richard's shoulder.

"Dr. Chase? Good morning. My name is Candice. I'll be looking after you today. How do you feel?"

Through half-open, bleary eyes, he glanced at the tray of food at his bedside and the emaciated, old man lying crooked in the steel-framed bed to his right.

"Hospital?"

"Yes."

Richard looked around. Faded yellow walls surrounded him. A tiny television hung in the corner. To his left, beige blinds, crooked and half open, partially covered a large window. The old man wriggled in the bed and weakly coughed up a puddle of phlegm.

Candice smiled. "Go on, try to have some breakfast."

A hazy image of a little girl and screaming people flashed in his mind. He grabbed the nurse's hand.

"What happened?"

Candice looked away. "The doctor will soon be in to see you."

Before he could respond, she was gone. He pushed the food away and looked out the window.

Two hours later, a small, slightly hunched-over man in an

163

oversized, ill-fitting gray suit interrupted Richard's blank stare at the television. He introduced himself as Dr. Rodriquez, a psychiatrist. Richard stared past him, saying nothing, too afraid to ask.

"Richard, I'd like to ask you a few questions."

Dr. Rodriquez spoke slowly, softly. An accident had occurred. A child was hit.

"A *child*?"

"I'm sorry, Richard. She didn't suffer. I'm terribly sorry."

He stared at the doctor, still and silent. Tears poured from his eyes.

"Do you remember—?"

"Please go away."

Richard curled up in a ball and pulled the covers over his head. He squeezed his eyes shut and tried to block out all thoughts, but nothing would stop the horrific visions.

Ten minutes later, another physician came to his bedside. Dr. Tang gently pulled back the covers from Richard's face.

"Dr. Chase, your wife just called. I told her you were okay. She said she'd be in to visit later this afternoon."

He said nothing.

Go away, everyone, everything. Please go away.

An hour later, he caught a glimpse from his window of a small sliver of the Charles River shimmering in scattered rays of sunlight. He asked the nurse when he would be discharged.

"Today, after you see the social worker and Dr. Rodriquez."

A few minutes later, he threw on his wrinkled shirt and pants, checked the hallway for his nurse, and disappeared down the back stairs. Twenty minutes later, his cab pulled into the marina. His boat would be ready in two hours.

An unseasonably cool, early September breeze blew at the waterfront. Gray clouds filled the sky. The boat-hand looked Richard over.

"Sure you want to go out in this weather? It looks like we may be getting some rain later."

He looked away. "I'm only going out for an hour or so. I'll stay close to shore."

Richard headed out in his twenty-one-foot powerboat, cruising at ten knots. For two hours, he maintained a steady course out to sea. The skyline of buildings, more than twenty miles behind him, had long since disappeared from view. The sky darkened and a light drizzle began to fall. He cut the engine. Time seemed to vanish. He slumped onto a swivel seat at the back of the boat, peered out at the infinite mass of churning black water, and fell into a trance.

The little girl looked up at him, her sweet face contorted in pain and disbelief. Blood oozed from her ear and nose, staining her pretty white tennis outfit. Her whimpering mother rocked the dying child in her arms. Leslie and Justin's shocked faces looked on.

Richard shook his head and wiped the ocean spray from his eyes, but the faces only intensified. He stood up and cried out. A rush of nausea and dizziness dropped him to his knees. He vomited, his bilious insides splashing onto his hands and coloring the water at his feet. He lifted his head toward the gray sky, shook his raised fists, and screamed. The wind and waves and vast emptiness swallowed up his fury, reducing it to an inconsequential whimper. He raised his arms higher and screamed louder. The rain fell, the wind blew, the water churned. He groaned weakly and collapsed into the puddle at the bottom of the boat. He closed his eyes and wished for sleep, but sleep wouldn't come, kept away by his parched mouth, shivering, and the horrific spectacle of face after face after face. He squeezed his eyes shut.

Please stop, please stop, please stop.

But images from the past kept appearing.

He found himself sitting at the kitchen table in the dark of the early morning, legs dangling above the floor, eating breakfast with Mom and Dad. They were quiet. Dad had his work clothes on. Little Richard heard the wind howling and the freezing rain coming down in sheets. The electricity was out. Dad was leaving to fix the electrical poles far away. He told Mom he would be gone a few days.

Dad bent over to hug him. Richard buried his nose in his dad's shirt, taking in the comforting, familiar odor. Richard looked at his mother. She was always sad, but she was sadder than usual when he left. She swallowed a handful of pills.

Later, a strange man came to their house and told Mom something. She fell to her knees and screamed. The man said it wasn't Dad's fault. A high-voltage wire had come loose and touched him.

Richard thrust open his eyes to rid himself of these nightmarish scenes, but they only intensified.

He stood at his mother's bedroom door. She sat cross-legged on the bed with a brown bag and a red tin can with a spout. She was crying. Richard ran toward her, but she stopped him with a wave of her arm, holding the container. A stream of gasoline flew across the room, burning his young nostrils. She dropped the bag full of insurance money. She soaked the money with the gasoline and lit a match. A huge flash and a shocking heat kicked him back into the hall. He rushed in with water, but it was too late. He dropped to his knees and screamed and screamed.

Large, flat-crested waves, one after the other, slapped the side of the rocking boat, soaking him with a spray of cold saltwater.

He crept upstairs after hearing a sound from Justin's room, shocked to find him in his bed under the covers. No movement. Was he asleep? What the hell was he doing home at this time? Could he have heard something, or worse, seen them on the couch? Might his son have heard her voice? Richard rushed downstairs in a silent panic, whispering to her to remain quiet, that his son was upstairs, that they've got to get out of there before he awakes.

Richard buried his face deep into his cold, wet hands. *Please stop. Leave me alone. Please.*
Twenty miles offshore in the black of night, with his tailbone soaking in frigid water, his knees tucked into his

chest, and his teeth chattering, Richard began to sob. He looked into the cold night sky and saw nothing but blackness. His shattered mind could now only think of one thing.

A good place to die.

Loud screeches and squawks from seagulls announcing the first light of morning aroused Richard from a deep sleep. Through half-open, crusted eyes, he saw nothing but sky, framed by the sides of the boat rising up beside his head. He felt the bobbing of the boat and cold water soaking his neck and back. He tried to move, but couldn't. He closed his eyes and hoped for sleep.

A moment later, he was awoken again, this time by a bump on the side of the boat. He forced open his heavy eyes. A gaunt face with a scraggly gray beard looked down on him, frowning.

"Hey buddy, you okay?"

Richard leapt up and scurried on all fours away from his unexpected guest. He attempted to cry out, but his bone-dry, crusted mouth and throat could emit only an incomprehensible bleat.

"You okay? What you doing out here?"

Richard peered out over the expanse of water. "I . . . I don't know."

"What's your name?"

"Chase."

The fisherman removed his baseball cap and rubbed

his muscular, sunburned neck. "Hang on. I'll be back." He returned to his boat and came back with water, a first-aid kit, pillows, and dry blankets. Richard chugged a pint of water. He dug his water-soaked wallet out of his back pocket and handed it to his rescuer.

An hour later, an officer from the Coast Guard took Richard and his boat back to the harbor. His screaming thirst and coldness satiated, he surrendered to a deep sleep.

Richard awoke with a start as the nurse opened the drapes.

"Well, good morning. Welcome back to the land of the living. You slept the whole clock around. How do you feel?"

"Oh, God. What happened?"

"The Coast Guard scooped you out of the ocean yesterday morning, half dead. You're looking a lot better now. Your doctors should be in shortly. Oh, by the way, your wife visited yesterday when you were sleeping."

Richard closed his eyes and turned his head away. "Did she say anything?"

"Just asked how you were. She's been talking to the doctors. She said she'd be around to see you later this afternoon."

Later that morning, Richard saw the on-call family practice physician, had a long visit with Dr. Rodriguez, a meeting with social services, and was cleared for discharge.

At two thirty, a knock came at his door. Leslie approached the head of the bed. Deep creases lined her forehead. Dark circles sat under her sunken eyes. Her appearance shocked him. She forced a sad smile.

"How are you feeling?"

Richard looked past her, into the hallway, saying nothing.

"Come on, let's get you home."

They drove home in silence.

Leslie pulled into the driveway, barely missing the garbage can. "Go on in," she said, taking her cell phone out of her purse. "I'll be in in a second."

Richard dragged himself up his front steps, wondering what she must be thinking. Was she calling Justin? He walked into the kitchen and flopped down at the table. The big house was quiet as a tomb. The horrific events of the previous forty-eight hours once again raced through his mind. The sickening, dull thud of a metal bumper striking soft flesh shot through his body like a bolt of lightning.

Several minutes later, Leslie entered the kitchen. She made coffee, poured a cup for each of them, and sat down at the table. She pushed the cup toward him. "Justin is staying with his friend Alex for a little while."

Richard frowned. "Alex? Why? For how long?"

"A couple of weeks, I think. They're playing in a soccer tournament."

"How is he feeling?"

"I don't know, really. He's very quiet."

"Whose idea was it, for him to stay with Alex?"

"His. Well, he says Alex suggested it. It makes sense. He's about forty miles away. They have practices in the morning and games in the evening."

"Maybe I can go see him play."

She sighed. "I don't know. Maybe you should just give him a little space."

Richard grabbed her hand. "Les, is he trying to avoid me?"

She shrugged. "When it comes to you two, I just don't know. I think he's just a little overwhelmed, that's all. He was shocked, like everyone. He still is. Believe me, I'm sure he feels bad for you, in his own way. He said he'd be dropping in before the tournament is over. You guys can talk then."

He looked at her gloomily. "I hope so."

Richard brought the cup to his lips, allowing the steam to rise over his face. He took a tiny sip, barely enough to wet his lips, and put the cup down. He stared into the swirling black liquid until his vision became blurry. He turned his head away and wiped his eyes.

For the next several minutes, they sat at the table, silent and still, Richard looking at his coffee cup, Leslie staring out the window. The loud clang of the grandfather clock, announcing the top of the hour, broke the silence. Leslie stood up. "Why don't you go lie down for a while? Try to get some rest."

Richard spent most of the next three days alone in his office or taking long walks to nowhere in particular, dragging his feet as if he were shackled at the ankles. He stared at his phone, hoping for a call from Justin, but it never rang. He wanted to call his son, but decided against it. If he needed a little time alone, so be it. Leslie looked after him as if he were a hospice patient, quietly providing for all his needs, forcing the occasional smile, speaking softly.

How much did she know? If she knew something, she wasn't letting it show. He thought about his commitment to tell her everything after the tennis match. How he wished he had just gone home and spilled his guts to her.

That night, after returning from another long walk, Richard found Leslie sitting on the couch in the family room reading a magazine. He hesitated for a moment then approached her. "Les?" he asked in a raspy whisper.

She looked up from her magazine. "Yes?" she asked softly.

For a moment, they looked at each other, saying nothing. Richard felt a powerful urge to turn and flee. Instead, he moved toward her. "I was wondering if I could . . . if we could talk, for just a minute."

Leslie pitched the magazine onto the couch next to her and nodded. "Have a seat."

Richard stepped toward the couch, and then awkwardly pivoted to the recliner on the other side of the room. He faced her and cleared his throat. "I want to talk to you about that day, at the awards banquet."

Leslie sat still and quiet, looking directly at him, expressionless.

He shifted on the edge of his seat and cleared his throat again.

"Les, I . . . a couple of months ago . . . I did a terrible thing."

He waited. She said nothing.

"Remember that idea I had, to strike back at Lundh? Well, I'm afraid I . . ." He lowered his head. "I'm sorry, Les, I ended up doing it. The bugging. I know it was wrong, but I just couldn't help myself."

He braced for the worst. A few seconds later, a muffled sob broke the silence. He looked up at her. Her knees were pulled up to her chest. Her hands were locked behind her neck. Tears streamed down her cheeks.

"Les, that package he gave me on the podium . . . "

"The DVD," she whispered. "I know all about it."

His body stiffened. The dull thump of metal on flesh rippled through him again. "Les, I don't really know what else to say, except that I'm so sorry, more than you could know."

Leslie grimaced. "After everything I said to you." She fell back on the couch, covered her face in her hands, and wept.

Richard eased himself onto the couch next to her. He slowly reached out for her hand. She turned away.

"Les, I'm sorry," he said softly.

"Oh God, I'm so mixed up," she said, her voice quivering. "I feel so angry and so sorry for you, all at the same time. I don't know whether to hug you and comfort you or slap the taste right out of your mouth. I'm sorry; I'm trying not to be angry, after what happened in the parking lot. I know I need to be strong and supportive, but it's . . . I'm just having a hard time."

Richard looked down at his hands in his lap. "It's okay. I understand," he said, barely above a whisper.

"I just feel . . ." She shook her head, as if struggling to find the word. "I feel so *sad*. Not just for the little girl. For everybody—you, me, Justin, the little girl's parents, even that bastard Lundh."

Richard stared at the fireplace, saying nothing.

A few minutes later, Leslie squeezed his hand, pushed herself off the couch, and went upstairs to bed.

Richard lay awake most of the night, tossing and turning, trying to settle his scrambled mind. Incomprehensible, fragmented ruminations poured forth, as if multiple, slightly out of range radio stations were playing all at once, competing for a dominant voice. Through it all, that horrific moment continued to scorch his body and mind, over and over.

The next morning, the doorbell rang. Leslie escorted a deputy from the sheriff's office into the kitchen. Deputy Roper informed Richard and Leslie that the investigation of the parking lot accident had been completed. Roper handed Richard a citation charging him with improper backing and careless driving along with a subpoena to appear before a judge in twenty days for sentencing.

There were no criminal charges. No charge of reckless endangerment. The negative drug screen, negative blood alcohol level, and limited view afforded by the SUV were key mitigating factors. He was advised to have an attorney present. Numb, Richard stared blankly past the deputy and said nothing. Leslie wiped her eyes.

Later that afternoon, a heavy knock came at the door. Two grave-looking police officers looked back at Richard through the peephole. Leslie approached from the kitchen. Richard took a deep breath and opened the door.

"Richard Chase?"

"Yes?"

The officers entered, stopping in the foyer. "We have a warrant for your arrest."

Richard glanced at Leslie. Tears filled her eyes. He looked at the arresting officer and nodded.

"I understand, officer. I've been expecting you. I won't give you any trouble. Can I have a moment with my wife?"

Richard hugged her. At the moment of their contact, she burst into tears.

"It's okay, Les. I'll be okay. We knew this was coming, right?"

He pulled back and looked at her. Grief filled her face, but he could also see anger in her eyes. Her eyes frightened him.

"Les, I'm so sorry for all this. I promise, we'll be okay."

She nodded quickly and wiped her eyes. "Go on, they're waiting for you."

Richard was charged with two counts of burglary of an occupied dwelling and one count of unlawful interception of verbal communication. Leslie covered her mouth as he was handcuffed. He was booked, fingerprinted, and released on a fifty thousand dollar bond. They drove home in silence.

As they pulled into the driveway, they saw Justin sitting on the front steps, tossing a soccer ball in the air. Richard stiffened. He glanced at Leslie. She put the car into park and punched the foot brake down. "Looks like he's come home to see you."

"Does he know about Lundh?"

"No. We just talked about the accident."

Richard reached for the door handle. Leslie grabbed his wrist. "You do know he's going to find out, about the bugging."

He looked at her and sighed. "I know, but not today, okay?"

Leslie released his wrist. "Okay," she said softly.

Richard approached his son, his stomach tied up in knots. Waves of fear and guilt flooded over him. "Hi," he said, barely audible.

Justin tossed the ball into the yard. "Hi." His cell phone rang. He ignored it. "How was it, at the courthouse?"

"I have a court date in three weeks."

"What are they going to do? Going to lose your license? Go to jail or something?"

"I don't know."

Richard sat down next to his son. "Jus, I couldn't see her, behind the SUV."

"Yeah, I know. It was an accident. Could have happened to anybody. Mom told me."

Richard put his hand on Justin's knee. "Are you okay?"

Justin stood up and walked into the yard. "Yeah, I guess."

"How's the tournament going?"

"Okay. Still practicing. It starts next week."

"What are you playing?"

"Midfield, of course."

Richard smiled. "Of course. Good luck to you and Alex."

"Thanks."

"So, I'll see you later?"

"Yeah," he shouted, his back to his father.

Richard stood up and headed for the door.

"Hey Dad?"

Richard spun around. "Yeah?"

"I'm really sorry about the accident."

Richard nodded and pushed out a joyless smile. "Thank you, Son. I love you."

Richard spent most of the next week walking aimlessly in his neighborhood or sitting in the public library staring at his hands. In the first few days, Leslie had made several attempts to boost Richard's morale, but her despair only added to Richard's pain. At Leslie's insistence, he met with his attorney.

On the morning of his arraignment for the burglary,

Richard awoke early in a cold sweat. Later that morning, he stood before the judge.

"Mr. Chase, you have been charged with two counts of burglary and one count of violation of the state wiretapping law. How do you plead?"

The attorney answered, "My client pleads guilty on all counts, Your Honor."

Richard's sentencing date was set for fifteen days, provided the pre-sentencing investigation could be completed within that time. He silently left the courtroom with his head lowered. Leslie held him tightly by the arm, guiding him through the parking lot to their car, as if he were disabled. Once again, they drove home in silence, her hand resting on his knee.

Richard spent most of the next week walking around the city and talking to himself. Leslie made his meals, attended to his domestic needs, and offered quiet encouragement, but the thinly disguised anguish carved in her face pained him. He called his son twice, each time leaving a voicemail requesting a call back. On the third try, Justin answered.

"Hello."

"Justin, I'm so glad to hear your voice. How are you?"

"I'm okay. You?"

"I'm okay, I guess." Richard squeezed the phone, his mind racing. "How is the tournament going?"

"We lost in the quarter finals. I'm going to stay to watch the final on Saturday morning. Mom told me you had to go back to court."

"Yeah. I just had to meet with my lawyer and sign some papers."

"When do you find out what happens?"

"A couple of weeks, I think."

"Are you going to go to jail?"

Richard hesitated. "I don't know. I hope not."

"I mean, I don't get it. It's not like you meant to—"

"I know, Son. Let's just see, okay? When are you coming home?"

"Saturday afternoon, after the final."

"Great. I'll see you then?"

"Yep."

Richard sat on the park bench wondering how long he could hold out before telling his son the truth.

Early Saturday morning, Richard rolled over in bed and gently nudged his wife. "Les, has Justin said anything about, you know, about what's been going on?"

"I think you better tell him. He's beginning to ask questions."

"What kind of questions?"

"Well, he's just wondering what's going on with all this legal stuff. He still thinks it's all related to the accident, but he's going to find out sooner or later."

"I know, I have to tell him. It's just not easy, that's all."

"Talk to him tonight. He'll be home for dinner."

Richard took a deep breath and rubbed his eyes. "Okay, I will."

Leslie made ricotta-free lasagna, Richard's favorite dish. Little was said during the meal, other than Justin's thoughts about a possible career in engineering. Richard complimented Leslie on the food, but secretly had to force it down. He had no appetite. He was only half done when Justin finished his plate.

"Hey Son, I was wondering if we could chat for a few minutes after dinner."

Justin glanced at his mother. "Yeah, okay."

Leslie stood up. "Why don't you two go out back? I'll bring you dessert."

They sat opposite each other at a poker table on the porch. Richard sat on the edge of his seat. Justin slumped back, looking into his lap.

"I want to bring you up to date about what's been going on with me."

"About what's going to happen to you?"

"Well, no, not really. You see . . . I'm afraid I did a terrible thing a couple of months ago."

Justin frowned. "Terrible thing? What?"

Richard looked away from his son, unable to speak.

Justin sat up. His eyes narrowed. "What did you do?"

"It's a bit of a story. I'll try to be brief." He glanced at Leslie cleaning up the dishes in the kitchen. She returned a reassuring nod.

"You know that endoscopy center I've always wanted to open? You know, my own little mini hospital where I can do my own procedures and be my own boss?"

"Yeah. You used to talk about it with Mom all the time. You called it a dream come true."

"Yeah, well the dream is long gone."

"Why?"

"One of the surgeons at the hospital became very angry with me for saying he was doing a bad job on his patients. To get back at me, he said some terrible things—all lies—to my financial backer, the person who was going to give me a lot of money to open my endoscopy center. Because of what that doctor said, the guy with the money pulled out and my dream went up in smoke."

"Wow. What did he say?"

"You know how strongly I feel about the Iraq war? Well, he told him about my 'extreme' views and claimed I said a whole bunch of terrible things to military families in the hospital about the war, which, of course, I didn't. As it turns out, the money guy is a strong supporter of the war, got really angry about it all, and told me to take a hike."

"Couldn't you talk to him, to set the record straight?"

"No. I tried, but he wouldn't take my call. The damage was done anyway. I couldn't do a thing about it."

Justin moved to the edge of his seat. "So what did you do?"

"I got angry as hell, more angry than I'd ever been in my entire life." He took a deep breath. "Then I did something *incredibly* foolish, something I'll regret for the rest of my days. What I'm about to tell you . . . I've only shared this with Mom. Please keep it to yourself, out of respect for the doctor and his family."

Justin frowned. "Yeah, sure. So what did you do?"

"I bugged his house with a video camera."

"What? His house? Why?"

"To catch him in bed with his girlfriend, and then show it to his wife."

Justin's eyes widened. "Holy shit!"

Richard looked at his son. "I've never been so ashamed in my life."

"You actually did that?"

"I can hardly believe it myself."

"And you got caught."

"Yes. I got caught."

"Is that what all this lawyer stuff is about?"

"Some of it. I'm afraid so."

"You going to go to jail?"

"I don't know. Maybe."

Justin shook his head in amazement. "How could you do something like that?"

"I don't know. The rage that was boiling inside me . . . I just lost control. It's like I was . . . hypnotized by my own anger."

"When did you find out about this? When did you get caught?"

Richard hesitated. "Two, three weeks ago."

Justin leaned forward. "It was at the awards ceremony, wasn't it? I saw Mom running around the club looking for you, before the accident. She looked worried as hell, now that I think of it. I bet you found out and got all freaked out. Is that why you hit the kid?"

Richard shook his head rapidly. "No, I mean, yeah, I was upset, but—"

"So it *wasn't* an accident. You were probably freaking out in the car."

"No, Justin, it wasn't like that."

Justin jumped up. "Why didn't you just tell me the truth in the first place?"

"Justin, I—"

"You want to know something? You're pathetic."

Justin went into the house, slamming shut the sliding doors, causing one of them to jump out of the track. Richard chased his son inside, but he was already gone.

"Leslie, I—"

"I heard everything. It's okay. You did the best you could. He'll calm down."

—⚹—

For the next three days, as Richard waited for his sentencing for the accident, he barely came out of his bedroom. The night before his court appearance, his nightmares returned. From high above the car, he watched the little girl wander toward the back bumper. He cried out, but it was too late. The horrible impact jolted him awake, his body drenched in sweat. He reached out for Leslie. She slept peacefully, her head buried in a mass of curls. He kissed her on the shoulder, got up, and sat in a chair facing their bedroom window.

The next morning, Richard scanned the courtroom and found Leslie sitting in the back row. He also saw the dead child's parents. The anger in their eyes hit him like a savage punch in the gut.

The judge addressed the court. "Before I hand down the sentence, do you or your client have anything you wish to say?"

Richard pushed himself to his feet and faced the judge.

"Your Honor, I'm deeply sorry. I didn't see her. I wish I could . . ." He lowered his head and sat back down. He wished the mother had a gun.

Richard was formally charged with improper backing and careless driving, fined five hundred dollars, charged three points on his license, and ordered to take a comprehensive driver's education course within ninety days.

The mother jumped up. "Bastard! Murderer! You killed my daughter!"

The words thundered through the room, scorching him with pain and fear. His eyes filled with tears. He was told to step away. He could barely move. Leslie escorted him out of the courtroom as if he were blind.

With his final court date looming in just two days, when he would be sentenced for crimes against Lundh, Richard met with his attorney, James Cross. During one particularly unproductive session, Cross shook his head and looked up at the ceiling.

"Dammit, Richard, you're going to have to start showing a little interest here. I'm trying to help you."

Richard shrugged. "I'll try."

On the morning of the sentencing, Cross gave Richard last-minute instructions outside the courtroom. Richard didn't hear a thing.

The prosecuting attorney spoke first, followed by a few carefully chosen words by Cross. "No prior convictions . . . nonviolent crime . . . other tragic circumstances . . . physician . . . teenage son . . . no threat to society . . ."

The little girl's motionless, broken body flashed before Richard's eyes. He turned his head away to extinguish the gruesome images, but to no avail. He turned to Leslie, who sat in the second row. She nodded and forced a smile.

The judge turned toward Richard. "Would the defendant like to say anything before sentencing?"

"No, Your Honor," Richard said quietly.

"I find the defendant guilty and sentence him to nine months in the county jail."

The two counts of burglary of an occupied dwelling had been reduced to two counts of malicious trespass. The one count of unlawful interception of verbal communication, which fell under the statute of wiretapping, was given a suspended sentence. Richard showed no emotion.

Cross gave Richard a discreet, congratulatory nod, gentle pat on the back, and a reassuring smile. "Listen, Richard, it could have been a lot worse. With good behavior, you could get out sooner."

Richard looked away and said nothing.

"Let me ask the judge for a few days to get your things in order."

"Don't bother."

The bailiff approached. Richard spotted Leslie at the back of the courtroom, her hands cupped around her nose and mouth. The bailiff's large, firm hand dropped onto Richard's shoulder.

"Time to go, Mr. Chase."

The five thirty, pre-dawn wake-up blast jolted Richard off his bunk. He strained to see his watch in the dusty blackness of his cell before remembering it had been removed right before he was strip-searched and became inmate 37212. A disgusting concoction of barely organic remnants, substituting for breakfast, would be served in the chow hall at the Suffolk County Jail in fifteen minutes.

Richard listened to his cellmate's urine stream splash into the filthy toilet bowl. He cringed at each break in the stream, imagining drops of foul-smelling piss splashing onto the disgusting seat and the gray cement floor. Joseph was a tall, muscular man of about forty, with a hardened face, rope-like veins in his forehead and neck, and crooked, yellow teeth. He zipped his fly, turned toward Richard, and scowled.

Richard didn't dare move from his bed. The morning after arriving ten days ago, he had quietly slipped out of bed and tiptoed to the putrid bowl in near darkness. He had begun to relieve himself when, all at once, large calloused hands grabbed his shoulders, rancid breath blew onto his neck, and a fully erect penis thrust against his partially bare buttocks. Richard sprang forward, bumping his knee on the bowl and striking his head on the cement wall. He jumped back to his bunk as if bitten by a rattler, amid howls of laughter from his new friend. Bursting bladder or not, he would wait his turn.

The cell block consisted of a gray cement and steel structure in the shape of an "H." Each of the four ends housed twelve, two-man cells, with each cell measuring ten-by-twelve feet, barely large enough for an old, cast-iron bunk bed with thin mattresses and two small lockers.

Richard was told to occupy the top bunk. Each of the four groups of cells in Richard's building had its own stainless-steel toilet and sink. Each inmate kept his own bar of soap, shampoo, and toothbrush in his locker.

Richard approached the bowl. Before initiating his stream, he took a quick look around. He saw nobody within striking distance.

Come on. Relax. There you go.

No amount of psychological preparation would have prepared him for life as an inmate. Every human contact, from the briefest, most indirect eye contact to a barely noticeable, accidental touch, was a potential time bomb. Every thought, every action—sitting quietly alone in the yard, talking to the guards, jamming himself between inmates in the mess hall for a few square inches of table space to endure his barely edible meal, or sweating through work detail—was dominated by an all-consuming need to be ready for "fight or flight."

Had he been raped, sodomized, or physically abused, as he had feared? Aside from the close call with his deranged bunkmate, no. But he had already had food repeatedly stolen from under his nose at dinner, and a homosexual in the dorm had openly propositioned him, repeatedly. He wondered how long he could last.

Suspicion, contempt, anger, and even hatred filled the air, but in the short time he had been there, he also had seen apathy and aloofness. Often, he felt as if he were invisible to the multitude of stone-cold robots looking right through him.

Richard returned to his bunk to retrieve his toothbrush. Never in his life had he placed such supreme value on an item of such inconsequential monetary significance until he'd had to do without it for a day.

A guard met him in the hallway.

"Chase, let's go!"

Richard's days were highly structured. All inmates at the facility had to choose either school or a work activity. Since his education precluded the school option, Richard was assigned to road crew and garbage dump. Every morning, following the head count after breakfast, he and about twenty others headed out to the road assignment for the day. His reward for a morning's work would be a disgusting bagged lunch—a tasteless cheese sandwich and a mushy brown banana—with the promise that if he did a good afternoon's work, he would receive a disgusting dinner—shriveled up pieces of pork and brown beans, both soaking in oil. Thank God for the canteen, where he could buy honeybuns and chocolate bars with what little money he was able to maintain in his account.

His only sustained leisure time during the week came after dinner, between seven and lockdown at ten. He would read a book or watch whatever was on television in the common area. Leslie had sent him a book on chess. He made a makeshift chessboard and pieces from a deck of cards he had bought from the canteen. Whenever he could, he would solve chess problems, work through famous games of the masters, and even play matches against himself sitting in his cell. In the yard, he would sit alone. Nobody bothered him.

His weekends were relatively free. If weather permitted, he tried to spend most of the time outside in the yard exercising, always being sure to avoid the others.

Two weeks after Richard arrived in prison, Leslie made her first contact visit, without any intervening bars or bulletproof glass. Her cheeks were more sunken. Had she lost weight? She still had dark circles under her eyes. She looked at him and tried to smile. "How are you doing in here?"

"Okay. As well as can be expected, I guess."

"Are you safe? I mean, you know, you hear all kinds of things."

Richard grinned. "I'm fine. Still a virgin, if that's what you mean." He hoped the joke would lighten her mood, but despite her attempt to conceal it, she couldn't hide the sadness in her face. "How's Justin?" he asked softly, looking away.

"He's okay. I've talked to him. He's calmed down a little. It's going to take time."

"Has he said anything about me?"

"He asked if you're okay."

"Good. I'm glad." He forced a smile.

Leslie shook her head and sighed. "I'm sorry, Richard. I just don't understand you two. I know he has the right to be upset, but it's like there is always something under the surface with you two, some mysterious weirdness."

Richard looked away. "Tell him I'm doing okay, and I love him. Tell him I'd love to see him."

Leslie nodded. "I will."

"So how are you doing? You look tired."

"One day at a time. I'm okay, really."

They passed the remaining time struggling with small talk. When their time was up, she gave him a sad smile and promised to visit as often as possible.

About a month later, shortly after he arrived back from his work detail, a guard handed Richard a summons. He sat on his bunk and opened the envelope with shaking fingers, glanced at the top of the first page, and groaned. Finally, the civil suit filed by the parents of little Amber Miller had arrived, as he knew it would. He stuffed the papers out of sight in his locker. He would need to tell Leslie.

By the following afternoon, Leslie had a new attorney picked out for him.

"Dr. Chase, after reviewing the essentials of the case, I'm afraid our challenge will be to minimize the financial damage in a bad situation."

Richard looked at him, stone-faced.

"Dr. Chase, do you understand what—"

"Yes, I understand. I'm sorry, but I'd rather not talk about it now."

That night, Richard lay awake in his bunk, looking up at the ceiling above his head. How could any amount of money, or anything else for that matter, make any difference to that poor child and her family?

Lundh suddenly flashed into his mind. Before the accident, the contemptible bastard had been his universe. But from the moment he ran over the little girl, Lundh was all but erased from Richard's consciousness. Even the arrest and sentencing for crimes against Lundh could barely keep him in Richard's mind. Now he found himself replaying the entire, horrible mess and the ferocious anger that had consumed him.

Where had that rage come from?

Richard stared frozen at the ceiling. Wasn't it obvious? He had been robbed of a dream, and viciously slandered. Yet a vague uneasiness began to settle over him. He had no doubt his anger had been justified, but his explanation—that Lundh had *led* him to this act of malicious vengeance, that Lundh had *made* him do it—gnawed at him.

If a hundred people had been in his exact situation with the same opportunity, would they all have felt and reacted in the same way? Hell, would anybody have done what he did?

How in the world had this happened?

What kind of person does this?

What kind of person am I?

He rolled over, shut his eyes, and begged for sleep.

The next morning, a brilliant, late-autumn sun greeted Richard in the yard as he filed out after breakfast. The unseasonably pleasant weather felt good. He peered through the layers of barbed and razor wire to a small grove of oaks and maples basking in the sun. He thought of how his own beautiful oak would playfully tap on the big window at home.

Richard headed to his favorite spot, a quiet corner next to a large maple by the fence. He had taken recently to cataloging the various types of grasses and weeds in the yard and making a detailed study of the intricate patterns of the razor wire. As he approached the tree, he discovered someone already sitting against the backside of the trunk, facing the fence. Richard turned around and sat down a short distance away.

A voice came from behind the tree.

"There's plenty of room for both of us."

Richard ignored the invitation. A moment later, a sound he hadn't heard for years filled his ears. A harmonica sang out from behind the maple. He listened to a novice but heartfelt version of "The House of the Rising Sun." The melody was played cautiously, mostly with single notes, awkwardly interrupted by a few chords. He strolled toward the fence to sneak a peek at this mystery musician. He stayed at the fence a few seconds, and then, pretending to have heard nothing, casually returned to his spot and sat down. The music started up again. "Catfish Blues," "Sally Mae," and "In the Wee Small Hours of the Morning" filled the air. This musician was no Junior Wells, but the playing was pretty damned good and a welcome diversion. Richard laid his head back, closed his eyes, and listened.

A few minutes later, Richard awoke, startled. He jumped to his feet. The musician stood before him.

"I'm sorry. I didn't mean to frighten you." The musician smiled and extended his hand. "Benjamin McGee."

Richard straightened his back. He silently chastised himself for getting caught. He had broken his own cardinal rule—ignore everyone. He glanced at the man standing before him. He appeared to be in his late forties, was tall and thin, had a narrow face, and receding straight black hair.

Richard felt his face flush. "I'm sorry, but I'd rather be left alone."

"You play harmonica?" McGee asked.

Richard looked at the trees. "I did play, years ago."

McGee smiled and extended his hand again. Richard hesitated, but shook it, using the formality as a way to announce his departure. He turned and walked away.

A moment later, Richard heard a soft thud behind him. He turned around and found a small, brown leather sack, dulled with age, lying at his feet. He picked up the bag, opened it, and found a tarnished Hohner Marine Band harmonica. He stuck the harmonica into his pocket and walked back to his cell.

That night, Richard lay awake in his bunk, staring at the black ceiling. His mind drifted back . . .

From outside the kitchen, eight-year-old Richard silently watched Dad and Grandpa Zach sitting around the kitchen table. Dad tuned his six-string acoustic guitar. Grandpa licked his old, weathered lips and blew chords into his gold-plated harmonica, eager to begin another Friday evening session of music, beer, and funny stories.

Grandpa Zack called Richard into the kitchen.

"Come here, young lad. Sit next to me."

A soda sat next to Grandpa's half-empty beer bottle. Richard watched in awe from his front-row seat. Grandpa winked at him as they played.

"So, young lad, let's have it. What've you learned?"

"Um, well, I . . . ."

"I thought so. Did you even notice how I hold the harmonica? How I shape my mouth? How I blow?"

Little Richard's eyes filled with tears.

Grandpa gave Richard a big bear hug, reached into his pocket, and handed the little boy a shiny, new silver harmonica.

"That's yours, my boy, for keeps. Welcome to the club."

Richard buried his nose in his grandfather's old overalls and hugged him with all his might.

The rest of the night belonged to Richard. He learned to play a few simple tunes. The grand finale came when the proud, new junior member played "Bye, Bye, Blackbird" solo. Little Richard took a bow. Dad and Grandpa applauded.

Richard could still smell his grandpa's shirt and overalls as if it were yesterday. Narrow streams of tears trickled down his temples into his ears.

Oh, God, how did I get from there to here?

He reached into his pocket and felt the smooth metal of the harmonica. How long had it been? He thought back to his college days, playing guitar and harmonica in a band. Why did he ever stop playing? He licked his lips and reached for the harmonica, but then stopped.

You can't bring back the past. Don't even try.

He wished he had never heard Ben play.

Richard awoke the next morning with the first hint of dawn. He listened for any signs of life. His bunkmate was snoring. Richard pulled the sheet over his head, brought the harmonica up to his dry lips, and blew into the harp, producing a full, warm C-chord. He fired it back into his pocket and held his breath. No response. He secretly celebrated.

The next day, Ben approached Richard in the yard.

"Hey, do you know how to bend notes? I can do it, but I'm having trouble."

Richard said nothing.

"Please? It won't take a minute."

Richard rubbed his temples and sighed. Persistent bastard, he thought. He dug the harmonica out of his pocket and licked his lips. "Alright, there's really nothing to it. You gotta listen to the sound and then just . . . Here, watch me."

The new pupil wasn't half bad. Before Richard knew it, they were laughing, joking, and playing music together. When it was time to go, Ben touched his mentor on the shoulder. "Same time tomorrow?" he asked with wide eyes and a smile.

Richard nodded and smiled. "Yeah, sure. Why not?"

A week later, Ben picked up his harmonica, and then put it down. The wrinkles in his face deepened.

"Richard, do you mind if I ask you something?"

"No. What is it?"

"It's about my situation, you know, why I'm here."

Richard shrugged. "I don't think you want any advice from me."

"I worked in advertising. Fourteen years. Loved my job. A year ago, I was laid off. 'An unfortunate victim of restructuring,' they said. I could take some bullshit severance package and hit the road or take a job transfer, doing the exact same thing for thirty percent less. I told my wife I wanted to tell them to shove their job; I got my pride. She got angry as hell. Who knows if I can get something else, she said. I told her the transfer was just a demeaning slap in the face, but she wouldn't buy it."

Richard stood up.

"Look, I'm sorry to hear about your job and wife problems, but I really can't help you."

"I was so pissed I couldn't see straight." Ben hesitated. "I tampered with the previous year's accounts receivable to set up the appearance of corporate tax fraud for the IRS. Problem is, I got caught red-handed, as they say. The judge gave me a heavy fine and a one-way ticket to this place for eight months. I lost my severance and pension. My wife and son, Eric, won't talk to me. For all I know, she's probably going to divorce me. Eric joined the military to get his education paid, and shipped out to the Middle East eight weeks ago. He wouldn't even shake my hand before he left."

Richard stiffened. "I'm sorry."

"I know I screwed up, Richard, but shit, I didn't deserve this."

Richard poked at the dirt. "Listen Ben, I don't know what to tell you. You were in a bad spot. What can I say?"

"I just wish Eric and Lorraine weren't so damned angry with me. It's like they don't want to understand. Man, I'd like to see them in my shoes for just a second."

Richard straightened and looked away.

Ben frowned. "What's wrong?"

"Let me ask you a simple question. This 'cooking the books' thing you did, why did you do it?"

"Why did I do it? I was angry as hell."

"Yeah, sure, but instead of the tax-fraud thing, why didn't you, I don't know, punch your boss in the mouth or shoot him or just quietly accept the severance and move on?"

"I don't know. At the time, it seemed like the right thing to do."

"Do you think everybody would have done what you did? You wished Lorraine or Eric could be in your shoes. Would they have done what you did? What about your buddies at work? Would they have done it?"

Ben jumped up. "What are you trying to say? I worked half my life for that fucking company."

"Okay, fine, you got screwed. But what you did, it was a *choice*. Stop blaming your actions on the situation and start taking some responsibility for what you did. It's nobody's fault but yours. Take some ownership. The sooner you face that, the better."

Ben's face flushed. "Thanks, Richard. Thanks a hell of a lot. See you around." He walked away.

35

The music sessions ceased. A week later, Richard considered approaching Ben to resume their meetings, but something inside told him to let it go. He felt he had already done more harm than good, for both of them.

He missed having a friend.

The following morning, Leslie showed up for her weekly visit. Her blond curls were now auburn. "How are things?" she asked, with a forced half smile.

"Okay, I guess. I like your hair."

"Thanks. Just thought I'd do something different."

"Justin okay?"

Leslie nodded. "He's fine."

Richard reached into his pocket and pulled out two letters. "Could you give him these? I was going to mail them, but I figured you could pass them on."

Leslie noticed neither letter was sealed.

"Feel free to read them, if you'd like."

"No, that's okay," she said softly.

Richard dove into his other pocket and pulled out the harmonica. "One of the inmates gave this to me."

Leslie smiled. "That's great. You haven't played in years."

"I know. It came back quick and easy." He hoped she

would ask him to play something, but she said nothing. He was about to offer, but decided against it. He flashed back to their honeymoon night, when he played a Donna Summer tune while making love to her. They had never laughed so hard in their lives.

He put the instrument back into his pocket.

"How is your painting?"

She shrugged. "I don't know. I'm just taking a break for a while. I got turned down for a major gallery showing, again. They don't even look at my work anymore."

Richard offered a sympathetic smile. "I'm sorry to hear that. Don't worry. One day, it'll happen for you." He hesitated, and then touched his wife on the elbow. "Hey Les? Are you doing okay?"

"I'm fine. I'll see you next week."

For the next month, Leslie continued to make her weekly visits, each like the previous one—minimal conversation, some encouragement, a few forced smiles, and a promise to return the following week. Could she ever forgive him? Richard didn't have the courage to ask. Perhaps she didn't know herself. Richard would inquire about Justin. Had he asked about his father? Did he want to come for a visit? Leslie would shake her head and shrug. Neither of them brought up anything about the surveillance or the accident. For that one hour each week, apart from the lines of despair on her face, the past had ceased to exist.

On a rainy fall morning, Richard dragged his feet into the visitor's room a few minutes late. He was exhausted, having slept poorly the previous several nights. He rubbed his eyes and yawned, looking for Leslie. She wasn't in the room. He frowned. She had always been there, waiting for him as he arrived. Something else must have come up, he figured.

He was about to leave the room when he froze. Out of the corner of his eye, he spotted his son standing in the corner, looking anxious and bewildered.

Richard ran to his son. "Justin!" Almost four months after his incarceration, his son had finally come to see him.

They sat down facing each other. Richard smiled a bittersweet half smile, the best he could give. "It's good to see you, Son."

Justin warily looked around the room at the other prisoners in their dark-blue prison uniforms. "So, this is jail."

"Well, yeah, I guess," Richard said, trying to hold his smile.

"So, what's it like to be in the slammer?"

Richard was hoping to see a hint of humor or perhaps a touch of sarcasm in his son's face. He saw neither.

"I've been in better hotels. This is the kind of place where you don't want room service."

Justin turned away, but not before his father could see a grin.

"How are you?"

Justin turned toward him. "I'm sorry for the way I acted, when you told me at home. It was still an accident, okay? I didn't mean to . . ."

"It's okay. Thanks."

Justin dropped his elbows onto his knees and looked at his feet. "I just can't believe you did that. I mean the bugging."

"Like I said, I was so angry, and something terrible just came over me."

Richard waited, but Justin said nothing.

"So, how are you doing at school? Last year, huh?"

Justin glanced at the large wall clock. "You look okay."

"I'm all right. Keeping my nose clean. Staying away from the bad guys."

Justin stood up. "Well, I guess I should go. I just came to tell you that."

Richard stayed in his chair. "We still got a few minutes. I want to ask about your mother. Is she doing okay?"

"Don't you see her almost every week?"

"Yeah, but, I'm just asking you."

"She's fucked up about all this, what you did."

"I know. Believe me, so am I."

Justin awkwardly looked at his watch. "I gotta go."

Richard stood up. "Thanks for coming." He touched his son on the shoulder. "Say hi to Mom."

Richard stood in the room, watching the visitors file out. His son had actually come to see him. Had Leslie forced him to visit? No matter; his son had come to see him.

He went back to his cell with a spring in his step.

The following week, on a cool, sunny afternoon, a pebble flew across Richard's chessboard. Ben stood before him with a timid smile. He reached into his pocket and pulled out his harmonica.

"Want to play?"

Richard grinned. "It's great to see you, my friend."

They shook hands.

"Richard, I'm sorry about the way I acted. I guess you didn't tell me what I wanted to hear. I was too busy feeling sorry for myself and blaming everyone else but me. It still stings like hell, but I guess I've just got to face it."

"Don't beat yourself up over it. This shit isn't easy. It takes a little time."

"You know, it's strange. I feel like I've traded anger for guilt. Anger's bad, but guilt . . . it almost seems worse. Maybe the truth's not always good to know."

Richard shrugged. "I don't know."

They started playing music again. They told stories and tried to laugh. Ben's mood gradually lightened, but he wasn't the same. Richard could see Ben's sadness following him around like a ball and chain.

One morning, several months after their reconciliation, Ben didn't show up for their usual get-together by the tree. Richard went looking in the yard, but couldn't find his friend. On the way back to his cell, he asked one of the guards.

"One of the inmates found him bashing his head against the cell bars about an hour ago. What a mess—his head all battered and bruised, nose broken, front teeth out. They transferred him out to the local hospital."

Richard could scarcely believe his ears. He raced around the yard trying to determine what had happened, but nobody else seemed to know anything. Finally, one of the other guards who sometimes watched Ben and Richard play their harmonicas pulled Richard aside.

"Poor bastard. A call came in from his brother a couple hours ago. His son got blown up by a land mine somewhere in Afghanistan last night and died. Warden gave him the news. He went back to his cell and started pounding his head against the bars, shouting, 'I killed him! I killed him!' You knew him pretty well, didn't you? Why would he say that?"

36

The next morning, Richard trudged back to his cell after breakfast and flopped down on the floor next to his bed. Try as he did, he couldn't stop imagining Ben slamming his head into the bars of his own cell to the point of unconsciousness.

Richard's own words haunted him.

Stop blaming your actions on the situation . . . start taking some responsibility . . . nobody's fault but yours.

He replayed Ben's own words over and over.

I feel like I've traded anger for guilt. Anger's bad, but guilt . . . it almost seems worse.

He buried his face in his hands.

By the time road duty came in early afternoon, Richard could barely lift his head off the pillow. He trudged along the side of the road, gathering up rain-soaked garbage, contemplating escape. Would they shoot him? He didn't much care.

For days, Richard pleaded with the guards for any information on Ben, but got nothing. He kept Ben's harmonica in his pocket, but he couldn't bring himself to play it. Finally, he asked one of the visiting chaplains to make a few calls.

"Bad concussion. He was unconscious for twenty-four

hours. He had a broken nose, some busted teeth, and a bad gash on his face. Twenty stitches. He must be doing better, though. They say he went home three days ago."

"Went *home*? But he wasn't finished with his time."

"He was granted parole. His sentence got reduced for special circumstances, you know, because his son died."

Richard had thirty-three days remaining on his nine-month sentence, which had been reduced to seven months for "good behavior." The thought of having over a month remaining in this hellhole seemed unbearable.

Leslie arrived late for her weekly visit. Greasy hair hung limply over her face. Dark rings wrapped around her eyes. A baggy T-shirt covered her emaciated frame. Could she have lost that much weight in a week?

Instead of diving into her usual routine of questions, she looked past her husband with red eyes.

"Leslie, what's wrong?"

"I've got something I need to tell you."

Richard felt the blood drain from his head. "What is it?"

"I found your briefcase, the one full of surveillance information."

Richard stared at her, puzzled.

"I found your secret phone, Richard. The one you never told me you had."

"Secret phone?"

"What were you doing with it?"

"I needed it to make anonymous calls to order the equipment and get it delivered—"

"And who else did you need it for? Who else were you calling?"

Richard shook his head. "Les, I—"

"Remember *Cathy*? I found multiple calls from you to her, from April the 5th to May the 23rd."

"Well, yeah, I told you I was helping her get over her divorce. I told you we were speaking for a couple of months."

"But why use your 007 spy phone? Why not use your usual phone? Wouldn't that have been a lot easier?"

"I don't know, Les. I guess I didn't want you to accidentally come across the number and jump to the wrong conclusion."

"Like I'm doing now?"

"Yes. Absolutely."

"So you've got nothing to hide?"

"Nothing. Like I told you—"

"Then how do you explain this?" She pulled a piece of paper out of her pocket and handed it to him.

"Thanks so much for the roses. They're beautiful. You didn't have to do that, but I appreciate it. I still think your idea is crazy and dangerous, so whatever you do, be careful. Talk to ya soon."

Richard caught his breath and frowned. "What is this?"

"It's on your secret spy phone, from that whore bitch, copied verbatim. I'd have you listen to it, but they won't let me bring in the phone."

"I don't understand. I never heard that—"

Leslie stood up. "Really? Come on! She was in on this bugging, wasn't she?"

Richard's heart pounded as if his head were about to blow clean off his shoulders. He wiped the sweat off his forehead and rubbed it on his pants. He lifted his head to look at her. "Yes," he whispered.

"Were you lying to me about your relationship?"

Richard shook his head. "No Les, I wasn't. I promise—"

"You promise? After what we've been through? Well I'm sorry, but I don't believe you." She fell back in her chair, covered her face, and began to sob.

Richard touched her hand. She yanked it away.

"Leslie, I needed help to copy his house keys. I wished it could have been you. I wanted it to be you more than anybody. But I knew that wasn't possible. I swear to you, nothing happened between us. I sent her the roses to show her my appreciation for copying the keys. She must have sent me that voicemail after getting them. I never heard it."

Leslie blew her nose and sighed forcefully. "I'm sorry to do this, Richard, but when you get out, I'd rather you didn't come home. I can help you find a place, if you can't do it from in here. I'm sorry, but this is all too much for me. I think I still love you, but right now I want to rip your throat out. I just need a little time to sort out how I feel."

She got up and left, leaving a pile of wet tissues on the chair.

Richard sat slumped in his chair, looking into his lap, until the bell rang.

The days crept by, painful and slow. He tried not to think of Leslie and Justin. He buried himself in his routine—eat, sleep, work, read, avoid others.

Finally, thirty-two days after Leslie's last nightmarish visit, Richard's last day came. On a cool, rainy morning, he strode through the gate back into the world, back to his freedom.

He didn't feel free.

He got into a taxi and instructed the driver to go to an address a guard had hastily found for him, just outside Boston. He texted Leslie and Justin to tell them he was out, but over the next twenty minutes, received no answer.

As the car flew through a driving rain, Richard pulled out a tiny scrap of old newspaper from his wallet.

"Driver? I'm sorry, can you stop at an ATM, and then go to this other place instead?"

Richard stepped out of the taxi. The rain had slowed to a drizzle. He peered at the two-story, red-brick house and double-checked the address. A dim, yellow light shone from behind the blinds in the front window. A late-model sedan was parked in the driveway. The lawn still showed the ravages of winter, with large patches of yellow, matted straw mixed with smaller islands of uncut new growth and weeds.

He tread up the uneven steps and rang the bell. No answer. He knocked a little louder. The door opened slowly.

Ben stood before him.

Richard could hardly believe this was the same man he had known in prison. Ben's cheekbones protruded below lifeless eyes. Long, thin hair hung over his temples and ears. His forehead displayed two vertical, reddish-brown scars, and his two front teeth were gone. He looked ten years older than in prison.

"Ben? How are you?"

Ben looked at him blankly and said nothing.

"Can I come in?"

Ben stepped back and silently motioned Richard inside. A musty odor assaulted his nose. He walked through the foyer into the dim family room. Heaps of clothes, dirty dishes, and empty food containers lay scattered over the floor and furniture.

Richard forced a smile. "I just got out today. You're my first stop. I wanted to see how you were doing, if you were okay."

Ben motioned him to a seat on the couch and left the room.

Richard moved a crumpled pair of jeans aside and sat stiffly on the edge of the couch. Dust particles filled the air, their random dance illuminated by dim light from a lamp next to the couch. The neck of an empty whiskey bottle poked through the cushions next to his leg. Wine cooler bottles, beer cans, and a large pizza box littered the room.

Ben reappeared with two beers and a bag of potato chips. He flopped down on the corner of the coffee table and emptied half his beer in a single gulp. Richard stared at the dirty, brown carpet between them.

"Ben, I, uh, I was shocked by the news. I'm so sorry about what happened."

"Yeah."

Richard looked around the room. "Where's Lorraine?"

Ben said nothing.

"How are you feeling, I mean, physically, you know, since your injury?"

Ben rose, removed a photograph from the wall, and handed it to Richard. It showed a handsome young man in cap and gown clutching his diploma and smiling. "High school graduation."

Richard's heart sank. Ben removed another photograph from the wall. A tall woman, smiling broadly, wearing a yellow summer dress, stood next to a red sports car.

Richard pushed a smile onto his face. "Nice. That's one fine-looking woman, if you don't mind me saying. She kind of looks like Audrey Hepburn, you know, when she was young." He glanced at Ben, hoping the compliment would bring a smile.

Ben showed no emotion.

"Nice convertible. Is that an MG?"

"Yep."

"Early '70's, maybe?"

"MG Midget 1970," he said with an impatient sigh.

"What's with all the ribbons on the door?"

"Breast cancer. Lorraine is a survivor."

Richard handed Ben the photo. "I can't imagine going through something like that."

Ben looked straight through him, as if he were invisible.

Richard's heart raced. He had always prided himself on his enviable skill of always finding just the right words when it really counted. Words, spoken sincerely and with compassion, always came so easily. Now his insides churned.

"She still drives it? I mean, it still runs?" He silently cursed himself for his awkwardness.

Ben looked at Richard, bemused. "All the way to California."

Richard widened his eyes. "California?"

"Left last week," Ben said, as if talking to himself.

"What? She went to California?"

"Yep."

"Why?"

Ben looked at him blankly.

"Jesus Ben, answer me! What the hell is she doing there at a time like this?"

"To get away from me."

Richard shook his head in disbelief. "I don't understand. Why would she go—?"

"She's gone to work in her sister's restaurant."

"Sister's restaurant? Where?"

"I don't know. Some fancy-ass place she owns south of L.A., on the water."

"When is she coming back?"

"Never, if she's smart." Ben stared at the photograph of his son.

Richard rested his hand gently on Ben's shoulder. "Ben, I know I never met Eric, but . . ."

The image of the little girl flashed into Richard's head, as real as if she were now lying dead before him at his feet. He stiffened and held his breath, waiting for the pain to subside. Ben said nothing, clutching the neck of his empty beer bottle with both hands, staring into space.

"Ben, what you said that day, when you heard the news . . ."

Ben looked at Richard with distant, empty eyes.

"Listen, you can't blame yourself. You've got to stop thinking—"

"Thinking what? The truth? That what I did got him killed?"

Richard jumped up. "For Christ's sake, Ben, you didn't get him killed. You had nothing to do with that. You didn't tell him to enlist. He could have lived at home, got a job, saved some money. He was a good student, wasn't he? He probably could have gotten some scholarship money."

Ben sprang out of his chair and shoved Richard down onto the couch. "It's his fault? Is that it? Is that what you're saying? Fuck you!"

"No! Of course not. All I'm saying is that his death is not your fault. Stop blaming yourself!"

An angry smile flashed across Ben's face. "Of course! How silly of me. Would you like another beer?" He went into the kitchen before Richard could answer.

Richard sat on the edge of the couch, staring at the dancing dust, clutching his half-empty beer. The rain had intensified, coming down in torrents, splashing onto the windows. A clap of thunder startled him.

How Ben had changed. Richard felt like an intruder in a strange man's house. Ben seemed to wear his guilt like a suit of armor. How do you cut through that? He thought of Amber Miller and finished his beer.

Ben reappeared and dropped a six-pack of cans onto the table. Before Richard could refuse, a beer was thrust into his hand. Ben opened his beer, shooting spray halfway across the room, took a large gulp, and slammed down the can.

"Now you listen to me, Richard. You can bullshit me until the cows come home. The bottom line is, if I hadn't done it, my son would be alive. I have to live with that, period. You have no idea how that feels. Don't feel bad about what you told me. Like I said, you were right."

"But I *wasn't* right. Please, just give me a chance to explain."

"Don't waste your breath. You can candy coat it all you want. It's not going to bring my boy back."

Amber Miller's face again flashed before Richard, scorching him with pain. But now, he didn't feel desperate enough to push it away. If Ben could only see Richard's bottom line—a *real* killing, next to his own.

"Ben, sit down. I need to tell you something."

"You don't need to tell me anything."

"I killed a ten-year-old child. I hit a little girl backing out of a parking lot because I wasn't paying attention. She died on the operating table."

Ben stood still, his eyes focused for the first time since Richard had arrived.

"I'm the child killer, Ben, not you. That's *my* nightmare, not yours. She wasn't my daughter, but after looking into the eyes of her parents, I wish I could trade my life for hers. That stuff I said in prison . . . I was just trying to make *me* feel better. The truth is, I deserve that kind of guilt, not you. See the difference?"

The two men stood before each other, silent and still. Richard searched Ben's eyes for understanding, but he saw only grief.

"Listen, Ben, I've got to get to my new place. Why don't you come with me? We can help each other."

"No, thank you. I'm okay here. You better get going."

Richard offered to stay longer, but Ben refused. Reluctantly, Richard called for a taxi. The two men walked outside onto the porch. They stood side by side, looking into the downpour, saying nothing.

Several minutes later, the taxi pulled up. Ben turned toward his visitor. "Listen, I want you to know, I'm sorry about what happened to you, with the girl."

"Just think about what I told you. I'll call you after I get settled."

Richard dashed down the steps into the driving rain.

Richard stood in a puddle before an old, weather-beaten, three-decker home off a narrow street in a working-class district just outside Boston. Cold rain came down in sheets, soaking him to the skin. Is this what the guard had found for him? Richard now wished he had paid more attention. He trudged up the steps, turned the knob on the peeling oak door, and entered. He passed through the foyer into a large room with two couches, some mismatched furniture, and a rolled-up carpet next to a staircase. An old man stood before a small television, watching hockey. Richard asked him where he could find the landlady. The man pointed down the hall without taking his eyes off the game.

Richard found an elderly woman with leathery skin and short, silver hair sitting at a table, engrossed in a crossword puzzle. Her large eyes darted above red-rimmed glasses.

"Can I help you?"

"My name's Chase. I . . . someone called to reserve a . . ." He looked around, bewildered.

She reached for a notebook in the pocket of her apron.

"Richard Chase. Let's see, the officer told me nine months for burglary. What did you do?"

Richard felt his face flush. "Is this really necessary?"

She smiled. "No, not at all. You can try down the street. Of course, not everybody takes ex-cons."

"I broke into somebody's house and videotaped him in his bedroom."

The old lady burst into laughter. Richard looked away.

The landlady struggled to her feet and motioned him upstairs. She showed Richard a small bedroom on the third floor with faded beige walls, a few sticks of old furniture, a worn rug, and a single bed in the corner.

"Facilities down the hall. Three hundred a month, up front."

He paid her in twenty-dollar bills. She counted the money, stuffed it into her pocket, and vanished down the creaky stairs.

Richard sat on the bed and almost sank to the floor. The room wasn't much better than the jail. He hadn't expected much, but he sure as hell thought he had seen the last of having to share the toilet. At least he could close the door and wipe his ass in private. He thought of going downstairs, getting his money back, and checking into a hotel, at least until he could find a better place, but he found himself suddenly overwhelmed by fatigue. Having sat down, he wasn't sure he had the strength to stand. At this point, he would have slept on a park bench. He'd give the place a day or two before doing anything.

His watch read three thirty, but it had water under the glass and had stopped. He crawled into bed and pulled the sheets up to his neck. He strained to look through the window. Wispy clouds raced past a brilliant half-moon. Six months ago, he couldn't wait to experience the joy of this first night out. Lying here now, he felt no such joy.

Maybe he should call Leslie, just to tell her he was settling into his new "home." He thought of Justin. Maybe he would try to reach him again tomorrow.

Memories flooded over him. He recalled crying when Justin was born, cutting the cord, and holding his pride and joy in his arms. He remembered pacing the hospital corridors, anguishing over the possibility that their eight-year-old little boy might have leukemia and the jubilation and relief of being told it was nothing more than a prolonged viral illness.

Richard tried to think of other moments in Justin's life—sporting events, birthdays, school activities, disappointments, accomplishments. But those memories seemed vague and distant. Ben had never run out of stories about his son while they sat in the prison yard. Where were Richard's memories?

Richard abruptly awoke at six thirty the next morning, startled by his new surroundings. He jumped out of bed and ran to the bathroom, but was too late; it was already occupied.

No damned different than prison.

He choked down a cup of burnt coffee, showered, and headed out to pick up a few necessities. Hopefully, the morning sun would dry his moist clothes. Perhaps later today he would find the nerve to call Leslie. And Justin. He also needed to call his attorney.

Richard spotted a gas station in the next block and decided he couldn't wait any longer to call home. But to his disappointment, both the home number and Leslie's cell phone went to voicemail. He left a message asking her if it were possible for him to pick a few things up from home sometime soon.

He called Justin's cell. Once again, he left a message. He reached into his pocket and found another number.

"Hey, Ben, it's Richard."

The line remained silent for a few seconds.

"Hello, Richard."

"How are you? How are you feeling?"

"Okay."

"I was thinking of coming to visit."

"No! I'm fine. I'm sorry, but I've got to go."

"Will you at least—?"

Richard's stomach ached. He sat in a nearby park for an hour, trying to keep his mind free and just look at the trees. He couldn't do either. He trudged home, barely lifting his feet over the cracked sidewalks.

He started up the steps to the front door when a horn honked from across the street. Leslie emerged from her SUV. Richard rushed down the stairs and across the street, oblivious to the traffic.

"Leslie!" He gave her a hug and a kiss on the cheek. "I'm so glad to see you. How are you? He glanced into the empty front seat. "How's Justin?"

"We're fine. And you? How are you?"

"I'm fine, just fine. It's great to see you."

Leslie opened the back hatch. "I brought over as much as I could."

Richard pulled out three large suitcases. "Thanks so much, Les. Have you got a minute? Can I show you my place?"

She looked awkwardly at her watch. "I'm afraid I'm late for an appointment. I'll give you a call."

She looked at the house and shook her head. "You know,

you didn't have to pick this place. I would have gotten you something better."

Richard smiled. "It'll do."

"I'll keep in touch. I promise."

Late the next morning, Richard decided to pay Ben another visit, once again unannounced. He knocked, rang the doorbell, and then peered through the front window. He saw nothing. He glanced at Ben's car in the driveway.

He took a deep breath and turned the knob. Here he was, breaking in again. He opened the door slowly and took a step inside.

"Ben?"

No answer. He looked everywhere in the house, but found only dirty dishes and empty beer bottles. He peered through the kitchen window at a large, above-ground pool in the backyard. He raced out to the pool.

Ben lay on his back on the pool bottom, an *empty* pool, thank God.

"Ben!" Richard got no response. He jumped into the pool and rushed to his friend's side. Ben's breathing was shallow and his pulse was rapid, but strong and regular.

What a mess! His matted, greasy hair hung over his face. He reeked of old sweat and beer. Richard shook Ben's limp figure. His head bobbed back and forth like a rag doll. A moment later, he opened his eyes, coughed weakly, and groaned.

"Ben, it's me, Richard! What the hell are you doing here?"

Ben looked blankly at Richard and belched. A gust of rancid, alcoholic breath kicked Richard back as if he had been hit by pepper spray. Richard promptly let go.

Ben staggered to his feet and grabbed onto the side of the pool, slightly bending the wall inward. "Oh, God. I'm gonna puke." Vomit splattered onto the sun-baked, light-blue surface.

Richard recoiled but couldn't escape being splashed. He jumped out of the pool, found a garden hose, washed his feet, and blasted Ben with a narrow stream of ice-cold water. Ben staggered toward the middle of the pool, covering his face. Richard burst out laughing.

At least the stupid bastard was alive.

"Stay put, for Christ's sake! I'm not finished hosing you down."

Ben looked up. "Richard?"

"Yeah, Ben, it's me, you stupid motherfucker. Look at you. You're covered in puke. Take off your clothes."

Ben looked at him stupidly. "Take off my clothes?"

"Everything. Hurry up. You stink to high heaven."

After struggling with his clothes, Ben turned toward Richard, hunched over and looking like a half-drowned rat.

"Jesus, Ben, what the hell are you trying to do, kill yourself? What's that going to solve?"

Standing hunched over in the center of the pool, his teeth chattering, Ben looked at Richard with empty eyes. Richard ran into the house and returned with three towels. He jumped back into the pool and wrapped them around Ben's shivering, naked body. With great difficulty, he managed to get Ben out of the pool and into his foul-smelling bed. Ben fell asleep before his head hit the pillow.

Richard washed himself and his clothes in the sink, threw on a pair of dry pants and a shirt from Ben's closet, and walked to the next-door neighbor's house.

"I'm a friend of your neighbor, Ben McGee. Do you know him?"

A tall man with a crew cut and white mustache peered over reading glasses.

"Ben? Yes, I know him. How can I help you?"

"I found him drunk in the bottom of his empty pool."

The man removed his glasses and shook his head. "Again? Oh man, that's a shame."

"What do you mean—*again*?"

"I found him there a couple of times myself. I can see the pool from my bedroom window. A couple of weeks ago, I saw him lying there, passed out, drunker than shit. I fished him out and slapped him silly. He promised he'd never do it again, but damned if I don't see him a few days later, laying there in the pool looking like a dead fish. I don't know if you know, but he's going through a pretty rough time. He just got out of prison. His son was killed overseas, and his wife left him."

"I know."

"Hell of a shame," the neighbor continued. "They always had so much fun in the pool, him and his son. Seemed like they were real close, you know? Now he just lies in there and gets drunk. It's a damned shame."

Richard checked on Ben, called a taxi, and went home.

That evening, he called his friend.

"Richard, for Christ's sake, I'm okay."

"Bullshit! You scared the shit out of me. What are you trying to do?"

"Look, I appreciate your concern, but I'd rather you just not visit anymore."

"Have you talked to Lorraine lately?"

"No."

"Is she coming back anytime soon?"

"If I were her, I wouldn't. Do me a favor, will you? Forget you ever met me."

"Could you give me her number? I want to speak to her. Just to tell her how you're doing."

"No! Leave her alone."

"Ben, I just want to—"

Before Richard could say another word, Ben ended the call.

Richard spent the evening staring out his bedroom window.

Justin can't stand me. Leslie wants to be alone. Even Ben doesn't want me.

He opened a bottle of scotch and drank himself to sleep.

Richard awoke at about five in the morning, his mind already racing. If only Lorraine knew about her husband's grief, the way he was living, his suffering. That might get her back. But if he couldn't speak to her, how was he going to—

He sprang out of bed.

I'll go find her.

At nine o'clock sharp, Richard called his parole officer and received clearance for the trip. He made his flight arrangements, got some money from the bank, and packed his bag. He wasn't sure if he was doing the right thing, but this much he knew—he owed his friend one more chance.

Richard arrived at Logan Airport at seven the following morning with a small suitcase and a carry-on. He boarded American Airlines Flight 145 and buckled himself into his window seat. As soon as they were airborne, he pulled out his long list of Italian restaurants south of L.A. on the coast, down to San Clemente. Which one could it be? If only he had more information.

He arrived in Newport Beach at three fifteen. He stopped at a hotel just off the freeway. The small room contained a double bed, tiny television, and bathroom. Finally, his own bathroom. He showered, shaved, and dressed in new clothes. He struggled with his tie. He couldn't remember the last time he had worn one. He obtained a map and outlined routes to each restaurant. Finally, he was ready. He headed out at seven.

Richard began with Cucina Siciliana.

"Hello. My name is Richard Chase. Could I speak to the manager please?"

He explained that he was a friend of the owner's sister, Lorraine McGee.

"No such owner here? Thanks, anyway."

At La Bella Napoli, Pasquale's, the Venetian, La Travattore, the Tuscan Garden, Antonelli's, Valencia's, La Bella Roma,

Corleone's Loft, and Sophia's, Richard received the same answer. He sat in Sophia's parking lot, rubbing his face in his hands. The three-hour time difference was beginning to take its toll. He had five more places to visit, all outside the immediate area. He pulled out and headed for the first place, B and R's Italian Bistro. He followed his directions, but became lost. He tossed the map onto the backseat in disgust and drove back to his hotel. He collapsed onto his bed, fully clothed, wondering why he had come.

Richard spent most of the next day watching television and ruminating while he waited for the dinner-shift staff to arrive at the restaurants. At six o'clock, he headed out, feeling hopeful. Camponeschi, Ditirambo, Armando, Maccheroni, and Gusto. Managers and owners all shook their heads. Nobody could help him. As the manager from the last restaurant walked away, he pulled out the list and ripped it into bits.

His hard work had accomplished nothing.

Richard headed for the restaurant bar. He ordered a double gin and tonic, finished it in a flash, and ordered another. He ordered a third during his meal and downed it in two gulps. The alcohol hit his brain like a freight train.

He paid the bill and staggered to the men's room. He listed forward on rubbery legs at the urinal, accidentally bumping his forehead into the shiny tile wall. He imagined Ben slamming his head into the bars, lacerating his face, chipping his teeth, fracturing his nose, slumping to the floor, wanting to die. Richard smacked his forehead into the wall a little harder. His eyes watered. He smacked his forehead yet again, much harder. Stupendous pain shot through his head and neck, obliterating his other senses. He dropped to his knees and vomited his gin-soaked dinner into the bowl. The automatic urinal flushed, sending a spray of icy cold water and alcohol-soaked projectiles onto his face. He stumbled to the sink and immersed his head under cold water. The bathroom door opened. He flew into a stall, collapsed onto the seat, and hung his head between his legs.

Look at you. Just like him.

After sitting in the stall for about twenty minutes, Richard cleaned himself up as best he could and headed for the entrance. He grabbed his keys, stopped, and turned to the receptionist. "Excuse me. Can you call a taxi please?"

A pretty young woman looked up from her reservation list, sprang out from behind her podium, and led him into the lobby next to the entrance. "Sure, we can do that. Here, come and sit down. You okay? You want some water?"

Richard nodded.

The receptionist returned with the manager he had previously seen and a glass of ice water. "Sir, are you feeling okay?"

Richard took a small sip of water and burped. The taste of vomit and booze filled his mouth. "I'm okay," he said in a hoarse whisper. He thought of the mess he must have left. "I'm sorry for the mess in the bathroom."

"Do you have a car here?"

Richard nodded. "I'll come and get it in the morning."

"Megan will let you know when the taxi is here."

"Thanks."

Richard fell back into his chair. He looked at his watch. Almost ten and the place was still so busy. A fierce headache began pounding over his eyes. His joints ached. He felt as if he hadn't slept for days. He brought the glass up to his lips but reconsidered. Another one of those putrid burps might set him off vomiting again.

As he sat in the chair rubbing his temples, waves of bitter disappointment once again came over him. How had he not found her? He was sure he had checked every single Italian restaurant in the area, from south L.A. halfway to San Diego. Had Ben given him bad information? Perhaps he should try to—"

Megan approached him. "Sir, your taxi is here." She walked him to the entrance. A light rain fell. "He's around the corner in the parking lot to the left."

"Thank you. I'm sorry for the trouble."

She smiled. "No trouble at all. We're glad you're doing the right thing. Take care."

Richard stepped into the rainy night and laughed a bitter, angry laugh.

The right thing? Is that what I'm doing? Chasing halfway across the country looking for somebody who probably doesn't want to see me, to help somebody who doesn't want to be helped?

Rolling thunder filled the western sky from over the water. A light drizzle suddenly became a heavy downpour. Richard spotted the bright-yellow taxi and ran toward it, dodging between expensive cars in the parking lot. In his haste, he accidentally clipped a driver's side mirror of a luxury SUV, collapsing it inward. He swung around and popped it open.

He started heading for the taxi, and then stopped abruptly. The rain now flooded down in sheets, soaking his face. The taxi driver honked his horn. Richard didn't hear the honk. He didn't feel the torrential rain soaking his skin. He didn't see the flash of lightning over the ocean lighting up the coast.

Before him, in the corner of the crowded parking lot, he stared at a bright-red sports car.

Richard approached the tiny MG as if he were sneaking up on a sleeping tiger, his feet soaked to the ankles, his pants sticking to his wet skin. He flashed back to the photograph Ben had shown him, dashed to the car, and looked at the driver's door.

Three breast cancer ribbons.

He put his cold, wet hands to his mouth and stared at the car, disbelieving. Tears filled his eyes.

The taxi pulled up next to him and rolled down his window an inch. "Hey buddy, you call for the taxi? Let's go."

Richard looked at the driver, then the MG, and then jumped into the taxi. He wiped his eyes with wet fingers. "Could you just drive around the block a couple of times until I decide what to do? Or maybe just sit here? Don't worry, I'll pay you for your time."

The driver frowned and shook his head. "Whatever, it's your dime."

They drove down a couple of blocks and back. Before they had returned to the restaurant for the second time, Richard made a decision.

"That will be great. Just let me off at the parking lot."

"Buddy, you don't look ready to drive."

"I'm not," he shouted, laughing, as if the cabbie had just told a good joke. "I'm going back into the restaurant. Thanks for your help."

Richard jumped out of the cab, slapped the door twice, and watched the bewildered cabbie drive off. He turned toward the restaurant, stopped, shook his head, and went to his car. What was he thinking? He couldn't just walk back in there now, smelling like a distillery, and expect the manager to introduce him to Lorraine, especially after his mess in the bathroom. No, he needed some time to figure this out. He had come this far. He didn't want to mess it up now.

Richard moved his vehicle to within sight of the MG. He turned on the heat, hoping it would dry him out a little. Instead, the rental car began smelling like a musty old ashtray. His headache returned, worse than before. He wondered if he might vomit again.

He was in no shape to see her this evening. Unfortunately, only one option remained. He would follow her home and pay her an unexpected visit tomorrow. He had hoped for a less-intrusive meeting, but hey, what was he complaining about? A few minutes ago, he thought it was all over.

Richard shook his fists and rejoiced. Finally, he had found the elusive Lorraine McGee. Crouched down in his seat, soaked to the skin, smelling of booze, vomit, and tobacco, feeling exhausted and still a little drunk, he waited for Lorraine.

He would wait all night if he had to.

He never felt better.

The following afternoon, Richard pulled up to a two-story, Mediterranean-style home centered on a large, meticulously landscaped property. He glanced at the black BMW convertible in the driveway. The restaurant business must be good, he thought. He took a deep breath and looked into the rearview mirror—tasteful clothes, fresh shave, haircut. He was ready.

He strode up to the wood porch and rang the bell. An attractive, middle-aged woman wearing sunglasses and a sunbonnet appeared from the side of the house.

"Hello, can I help you?"

"Good afternoon. My name is Richard Chase."

The front door opened, and another woman appeared.

"Good afternoon, ladies. I'm looking for Lorraine McGee."

The woman in the doorway frowned.

"I'm Lorraine. How can I help you?"

"My name is Richard Chase." He hesitated. "I'm a friend of Ben's."

Lorraine's sister turned and walked away.

Lorraine peered warily at Richard. "Are you a lawyer?"

"No, no. I'm a friend."

"Did he send you here?"

"No, not at all. He doesn't know I'm here. But he is the

reason I've come to see you. I would like to talk to you, for just a few minutes, if possible."

"Is he okay?"

"Well, yes and no."

"You came all the way from Boston?"

"Yes, I did."

She sighed. "Come in. We can sit on the patio in the back."

Lorraine brought out a pitcher of iced tea and filled two glasses. Richard took a large sip. She ignored her drink and sat motionless, watching him with piercing eyes. Richard had rehearsed what he was going to say, and now he couldn't remember a word.

"Mrs. McGee, first I want to offer you my sincere condolences over your loss."

Grief filled her face. She looked away. "Thank you."

Richard told her how he and Ben had met in prison and the events leading up to the last time they had seen each other.

Lorraine finished her drink in one gulp and poured herself another, ignoring his empty glass. "So what do you want from me? What do you expect me to do, go running back to Boston to clean up the house?"

Richard leaned forward. "Lorraine, he's in trouble. If he doesn't get some help, I'm afraid of what will happen."

"Oh, please!"

Richard stood up. "Lorraine, he's *dying*. His guilt is like a cancer. It's eating him alive."

Lorraine slammed her hand on the table, shaking the half-full pitcher.

"Yeah, well, he was my son, too. What about my pain and suffering?"

"Please, I'm just—"

"I know Ben didn't do it directly. He didn't ask Eric to join the army. He didn't plant the land mine. But you know what? When you boil it all down, it always comes to the same thing: If he hadn't done this terrible, illegal, selfish thing, my son would still be alive." She wiped her eyes and picked up the pitcher. "I think it's time you left now. I'm sorry you came all the way out here just for this."

"Oh, so that's it? He makes a mistake, and you crucify him for it? Punish him until the day he dies? Is that how you feel?"

"Is that how *I* feel? You have no idea how I feel. Tell me, have you lost a son or daughter, Mr. Chase?"

Richard lowered his eyes. "No."

"How dare you come here and tell me how I should feel or what I should do. 'He feels bad, he feels guilty.' I know that. Damn it, he should feel guilty. Guilty as hell! Go home. And stop talking about things you know nothing about."

A rush of heat came into Richard's face. "I came here, all the way from Boston, because I give a shit about your husband. Yes, he did a stupid, selfish thing. But for him, it's way more than that. He feels like he *killed* Eric, killed him with his bare hands. And it's slowly killing him. Can you even begin to imagine how *that* must feel? Not just to lose a child, but to feel that you did it yourself? Is there any wonder why he lies around drunk all day, not caring whether he lives or dies?"

"I don't need this shit! Leave now, or I'll call the police."

Jessie emerged from the kitchen and stepped between them. "Get out of my house, now! I'm calling the cops." She took Lorraine gently by the hand. "Come on inside, dear."

Richard stepped toward the patio door. "Lorraine, listen

to me, please! I know you're suffering, but his life is in your hands."

Jessie glared at him. "Who the hell do you think you are? How dare you? What gives you the right to—?"

"I have the right! He came to me for help. He trusted me. And what did I do? I failed him. I don't give a shit what crime he did. He deserves better."

"She lost her only son, for God's sake. What the hell is wrong with you?"

Lorraine flopped down on a patio chair and began sobbing. Richard sat in front of her.

"Lorraine, listen to me. I killed a child backing out of a parking lot, a cute, little ten-year-old girl, while her parents watched. It was my fault. I wasn't paying attention. She wasn't my daughter, but until the day I die, I'll always live with the horrible guilt of taking her life. It isn't quite the same, but please believe me, I know how he feels."

Lorraine lowered her hands onto her lap and stared at Richard, as if trying to understand what he had said.

"I'm begging you, Lorraine. Go to him. Convince him that he didn't kill his son. Grieve with him, for Christ's sake. Grieve with the only other person in the world who feels your pain the way you feel it. If the years you spent with Ben mean anything to you, you'll go to him."

She lowered her head. Tears trickled down her cheeks.

"Please, Lorraine, you're his only chance."

She bolted from her chair and ran into the house.

Jessie glared at Richard. "You get out of here. If either of us see or hear from you again, I'm going to have you arrested."

Richard spent the return flight the next day staring out his window. He turned down the beverage and miniature bag of nuts. To his right, an elderly man, smelling of cigars, was hunched over a magazine. Ordinarily, Richard would have initiated conversation. Now, he couldn't bear the thought of talking to anyone.

The awful realization of his failure grew with every mile.

He arrived home late and slept on top of the covers of his stale-smelling bed. He didn't stir until noon the next day. He looked out his dirty little window from his bed wondering if Ben were dead or alive.

Several hours later, Richard's taxi pulled into Ben's driveway. He rang the bell and knocked. No answer. Ben's car was gone. This time the door was locked. He ran to the back of the house and peered into the empty pool. He checked the back patio door. It also was locked.

Could he have gone to California? Perhaps he just went out to get more beer.

Richard walked to the neighbor's.

"He left yesterday. He went to his sister's place in Montreal."

"Montreal? Did he say anything about California or his wife?"

"No."

"Did he leave you a forwarding address or his sister's name?"

"I'm afraid not."

Richard walked away, promising himself he would finally stop this obsessive preoccupation. If the rest of the world didn't give a shit, why should he?

The time had come for him to take control of his own life.

41

Richard sat before his bedroom window and looked out at the dreary sky. He would sit here, all day, until he found a reason to leave. Cold, dark clouds raced past the window. Even the clouds had somewhere to go. Rain started to fall.

Three hours later, he threw on some clothes and headed out to visit his parole officer, Charles.

Richard recounted his trip to California. Charles listened without interruption. Richard took the list of job opportunities Charles offered, along with the name of a psychologist. They confirmed the date of the next mandatory visit. He left feeling a little brighter. Charles had become a friend, or at least as close to one as he had in the world right now.

Richard ate poorly, took long walks to nowhere, and endured restless nights filled with frightful dream fragments of the accident. A week crept by without a call from Leslie. He had called and texted Justin earlier in the week. No answer. Did his son know about Cathy? He had promised to take Charles's advice, but the job list and paper with the name of the therapist still lay untouched on his desk.

The next morning, he awoke at noon after a night of drinking and called the therapist, Leonard R. Randolph, Ph.D., for an emergency appointment. Dr. Randolph was a tall man of about fifty, with shortly cropped, reddish-brown hair and goatee. He wore black-rimmed glasses and had a permanent kindness etched in his face. Richard told him everything, unfiltered, as if reporting the news. Randolph listened intently, asked many questions, and outlined a broad strategy, including clarification of treatment expectations and goals. Richard agreed to a follow-up appointment the next week.

At the end of the next session, Richard informed Randolph there was nothing further to say. The catharsis had felt worthwhile, even a little comforting, but he saw no use in continuing.

Randolph laid his notebook on his lap and sat back.

"I understand how you feel, Richard, but with all due respect, from my side of the coffee table, I think we've just begun to scratch the surface. The real work has yet to begin."

Richard stood up. "Thank you for your time." He extended his hand. "If I change my mind, I'll let you know."

Randolph ignored his hand. "Can you give me at least two more minutes?" He pointed to Richard's chair. Reluctantly, his patient sat.

"You seem to have it all figured out for Ben. He's a good guy who made a few bad choices. What I don't get is why you insist on thinking you're any different. You made some bad choices and suddenly you're a monster?"

Richard headed for the door. "Thank you, Doctor. I've heard quite enough."

"What about your son?"

Richard stopped mid-stride. "What about him?"

"Don't wait for him to reach out. Go see him. I know you guys have talked, but you need to talk some more, a lot more. You can't hide forever."

Richard sat in his car staring at his phone. A few minutes later he called Justin. No answer. He left a voicemail.

"Hi Son. How are you? I was wondering if we could get together? It would be great to see you." He tossed his phone onto the passenger's front seat and drove off.

On his way home, he stopped by the parole office. Charles greeted him with a nod.

"See the therapist?"

"Yeah."

"How did it go?"

He shrugged.

"Going to keep seeing him?"

"I don't know."

Charles shifted in his seat. "Listen, I've been thinking about something that might interest you. It has to do with car safety."

Richard frowned. "What?"

"Please, just give me a second. I'm sure you know, some vehicles have a camera or some kind of sensor built into the back bumper."

"Jesus."

"A sensor that beeps or flashes a light if something is back there."

Richard sighed. "It wouldn't have made any difference, Charles."

"Maybe yes, maybe no. You don't know that. The point is, you think you're the only person who's accidentally backed into somebody they couldn't see? It probably happens more than you think. Anyway, I did some research. Rearview beepers or cameras are pretty uncommon. Their use is slowly increasing, but as of this year, they're still available on less than ten percent of new vehicles. I'm thinking, maybe if it were on more cars, especially SUVs, it could make a difference."

"I don't know. Listen, I'd better be going."

"Hang on. Maybe you could help raise some public awareness about it, you know, like seat belts."

Richard finished his tea with a gulp and left with a curt goodbye. As Richard drove home, his insides boiled. What was Charles thinking? Save a life? To replace the one Richard had killed, to make it all even?

Hell, why stop there? I'll save a bunch of cute little kids, so I can get myself into the plus column. If I can get enough little girl points, it'll bring her back, raise her from the dead. Then everything will be okay. I can see it now. By governor's decree, a life-sized statue of his eminence shall be erected in all the parking lots of the land, protecting the huddled masses as they scurry into their minivans and SUVs.

—◆—

The next morning, Richard went to the public library with his laptop. He owed Charles at least this much. He spent several hours on the Internet and made multiple phone calls. He was able to receive an e-mail from the National Safety Council in Itasca, Illinois, showing a table outlining statistics for vehicles involved in fatal crashes for the previous year. Total fatalities: roughly thirty-three thousand. Deaths associated with backing up: one hundred forty-five. Fatalities from backing up while leaving a parking space: thirty-five.

Thirty-five fatalities? Richard shook his head. The small number seemed to magnify his carelessness. Evidently, the rest of the world managed to avoid striking children in parking lots. A painful ache coursed through him. He regretted ever looking into the matter. He went home, vowing to forget the whole thing.

The next morning, he returned to the library. He wondered how many vehicles actually had some type of rear-bumper surveillance system. *Consumer Reports* revealed nothing, so he tried searching by manufacturer. Richard discovered only a few of the most expensive vehicles offered rear-detection devices as part of their navigation systems. He called several showroom managers and asked why more vehicles were not equipped with such a device. They all said cost was the issue. He called the Department of Safety and Quality Assurance at one of the major automakers in Detroit.

"Yes, we think it's an excellent feature and plan to introduce it on more of our vehicles if market forces and cost effectiveness studies are favorable."

Richard shook his head and sighed. The issue simply was not a public safety concern. Adding an expensive safety feature to all vehicles for the sake of a very select group of careless idiots didn't make any sense. He packed up and went home.

The common room was empty. Richard stretched out on the couch in front of the TV. Sleep began to overtake him, but he fought it off. He needed to complete his assignment. He opened a bottle of Merlot he had picked up on the way home and began in earnest on his laptop. An hour later, his letter to the editor—an impassioned plea from a tragic figure begging for the universal use of the rear bumper camera-detection devices—was finished. He called the editorial department at the local paper and faxed it.

All in all, a decent piece of work, he supposed. At least maybe Charles would be proud. He finished a second glass of wine, ordered a pizza, and fell asleep.

He awoke to a loud knock at the door. He jumped up and realized he didn't have any cash. Dammit, he would have to go to an ATM with the pizza guy. He wasn't about to let his dinner get away. He flung open the door, ready to plead his case.

Lorraine and Ben stood before him.

Richard stood in the doorway, unable to speak.

Ben stepped forward. "Well, aren't you going to let us in?"

Richard awkwardly motioned them inside. "Please come in."

The pizza delivery boy appeared on the steps. Richard reached for his wallet. "I'm sorry, I, uh . . . I need to go to an ATM."

Ben laughed. "Looks like we got here just in time."

He paid the boy and handed Richard his pizza. Richard tossed the big white box onto a nearby chair and escorted his guests into the common room.

Ben and Lorraine sat on an old beige, corduroy couch. Richard sat before them on an ancient green, velvet ottoman that smelled like cigarettes.

"Guess you're surprised to see us, huh?"

Richard stared at them. "Yeah, you could say that."

Lorraine grasped Richard's hand. "You should've seen me after you left. I was livid. I wanted you arrested. But then, well, it just hit me. I finally found him, in Montreal with his sister, drowning in Molson. I was frightened to death, but the second we saw each other . . ." Tears rolled down her cheeks. "We had cried together before at the funeral, but it wasn't the same.

I was so angry then. I wasn't crying *with* him. I hated him. But this time, we forgave each other, for everything. Finally, we could begin to share our grief. We could begin again, together."

Ben's eyes filled with tears. "You saved me, my friend," he said, his voice shaking. "I owe you my life."

Lorraine leaned over and kissed him on the cheek. "Please forgive me for the awful way I treated you. Richard Chase, you're a good man."

Ben headed to the front door. "I'll be right back." He returned a moment later with a large, gift-wrapped box.

Richard struggled with multiple layers of wrapping paper. He opened the beautiful leather case and gasped. A complete set of Hohner Deluxe Marine Band harmonicas lay before him. The full set—all twelve keys.

Ben smiled. "Top of the line for my favorite teacher. After all, it was the music that first brought us together, wasn't it?"

Richard stared through watery eyes at his gift and nodded, unable to speak.

"I sure as hell didn't know it then," Ben said, "but that day I met you in prison, that was one of the luckiest days of my life."

Lorraine stood. "We'd better go. We got a lot to do. We'll keep in touch."

Richard stood in the doorway and waved as their car pulled away. A smile swept across his face. He raced up the stairs to his room, taking three steps at a time. He hid the harmonicas, took one glorious leap, and belly flopped onto his bed. The defenseless relic came crashing down onto the old wood floor. He howled with laughter. He hoped the whole world heard the noise.

He felt the urge to run, and soon bounded down the stairs and out onto the sidewalk. He ran madly for seven blocks, gasping for breath and pouring sweat, until his heart threatened to burst out of his chest. People stared at him as if he were mad.

Look at me. You want to see me fly?

He was sure he could, but his exhausted body wouldn't allow another step. He found a bench and collapsed. He rested for a moment, and then took a running jump into a puddle left from the morning rain. Muddy water splashed onto his pants and shirt, even his face. He splashed with the joy of a child until the deep puddle was empty. He ran home with tears streaming down his face.

His landlord met him on the stairs.

"What happened to you? You're not coming in the house like that."

He laughed and ran up the stairs. He looked at himself in the cracked, full-length mirror behind the bedroom door. He hardly recognized the figure standing before him. Everything was different now.

If only Justin and Leslie could see him. He had wanted so desperately to put a smile on their faces, to show them a better side of himself. Lately, he didn't think there was a better side to show. But then, in the time it takes to answer the front door . . . He couldn't change the past, but maybe he could also do something for them, to show them, and himself, that he wasn't a lost cause.

He thought of Leslie's terrible struggle for recognition as a painter. If only he could somehow help her, if for no other reason than to make up for his tepid support over the years.

She wasn't lacking critical acclaim; she had received kudos from far and wide. Hell, even that old patient of his, who owned the gallery in Chicago, was crazy-impressed with that piece he had seen in Richard's office. The problem was—

Wait a second. That patient of his. What was his name?

Richard slapped the mirror with his muddy hand, leaving a conspicuous handprint, and laughed.

He had never felt cleaner.

The warm water in the shower felt wonderful. Who cared if the bathroom was down the hall? He thought about the pizza waiting for him downstairs, but decided to leave it for the house. Tonight, he would treat himself to a fine meal at the Charles Hotel in Cambridge.

He had so much to think about.

43

Charles led Richard into their meeting room.

"Back so soon?"

"I'm sorry for the other day. I acted like an idiot." Richard produced a folder. "Here, take a look."

Charles flipped through the documents and read Richard's letter to the editor.

"You did all this research and wrote this letter?"

Richard smiled. He told Charles about his visit from Ben and Lorraine.

Charles shook his hand.

"Congratulations. Have you told Leslie?"

"No, but funny you should mention her. I've got this idea, but I need your permission to travel again."

The following afternoon, Richard walked into the renowned Marcoux gallery, which specialized in traditional fine art and sculpture in the River North Gallery District of Chicago. He greeted the receptionist behind the marble counter.

"Hello. My name is Dr. Richard Chase. I have an appointment with Mr. Marcoux."

A moment later, Marcoux emerged from his office.

"The famous Dr. Chase, in the flesh! It's nice to see you again." They shook hands.

"Please call me Richard. I appreciate you seeing me."

"Thanks again for doing such a great job on me. Scary stuff, that pancreatitis. I never want to see the inside of an ICU again." Marcoux pointed to his office. "Shall we?"

They sat in a pair of straight-backed chairs next to an aquarium.

"I must say, Richard, you've roused my curiosity, coming all the way out here. How can I help you?"

"Remember the first time you saw me in my office, you commented on my wife's painting behind my desk?"

Marcoux smiled. "Sure, I remember it well."

"Well I'd like to talk to you about that."

Richard left the gallery an hour later, not knowing what to think. Marcoux had neither outwardly embraced nor rejected his request. All Richard could do now was wait and fight the growing urge to call Leslie. He knew it was important to respect her request for time alone. He would have left *himself* if he could have.

Nine days later, while sitting on a park bench, Richard's phone rang. His heart leapt when he recognized the Chicago area code.

"Richard, it's Lewis Marcoux. I just left your house. I must say, this body of work, I think it's quite extraordinary."

Richard sprang up.

"Really? Wow, that's fantastic. You didn't say anything to her, did you, I mean about my calling you?"

"Not a word."

"So what do you think? Can you help her out?"

"I think I can help us both out. I offered her a showing, and she accepted."

"You did what? You're kidding me. What did she say?"

"Say? She couldn't even speak. I've never seen a happier human being in my life."

Richard circled the park bench, unable to contain himself. "Lewis, I can't thank you enough. This is the break she needed."

"Hey, don't thank me. Thank yourself for helping to discover a great talent."

"So you're not doing this just for me, you know, because I took care of you?"

"You mean because you saved my life?" Marcoux chuckled. "No, Richard. Leslie's work deserves a showing. I'm happy to help you, but I'm pretty sure that if I'd stumbled upon her work myself, I'd feel the same way."

Richard thanked Marcoux again, ended the call, and shook his fists in triumph. Surely she'd call with her news before the night was through.

Ten days passed without a call. He found himself staring at the phone, willing it to ring.

The next morning, he reached for his phone on his bedside table.

"Hi Leslie. How are you?"

"I'm okay. How are you doing?"

"How's Justin?"

"He's fine. You managing okay?"

"Yeah. I guess. I've been trying to get my life back together. I miss you, Les." Richard waited. "Les?"

"I heard you."

"I was wondering, could I come over tonight? I'd like to pick up some clothes, and maybe a lamp and a few other things."

"Sure, I guess."

"Great. I'll see you around eight?"

"Okay."

He ended the call, sat on his bed, and waited for his pounding heart to settle.

At 7:45, Richard stepped out of the taxi and stood before the house he had lived in for twelve years. He reached for the door handle, and then stopped himself and rang the bell instead. Leslie motioned him inside.

The distinct scent of their favorite perfume swept over Richard. She wore a jean skirt and a lilac blouse, buttoned down just enough to be tastefully sensual. Richard glanced at her and felt a rush of desire. He hugged her tightly. She didn't pull away.

"Thanks for seeing me, Les."

Everything looked the same—the beige carpet, the gold-colored, faux-painted walls, Edward Hopper's *Nighthawks* above the upright Steinway, the framed photographs of the Grand Canyon, and Leslie's own landscapes. Even the piles of newspapers, magazines, and folded clothes scattered about seemed so familiar, it was as if he had just left that morning.

"Is Justin home?"

"No, he's off to the high school basketball game with his girlfriend. He'll probably be home at about midnight."

"Girlfriend?"

"He met her at a party. They've been together for about three months. Nice girl."

Leslie escorted him into the living room. They sat opposite each other, separated by their glass coffee table. He studied her face as she poured tea.

"Leslie, I want you to know, I'm really happy to see you."

She forced a half smile. "It's good to see you too. I'm glad you're doing okay." Her eyes suddenly became big. "Hey, I got some great news."

The telephone rang in the kitchen.

"I'm sorry. Hang on a second," she said, getting up.

"Take your time."

Richard wandered over to the fireplace. He looked at a painting of the three of them, titled *Trio,* done by Leslie five years ago from an old photograph. In the picture, Leslie and Richard were sitting on a loveseat, smiling at twelve-year-old Justin who sat between them, mugging for the camera. At least she hadn't taken the photo down.

A stack of gold envelopes rested on the fireplace mantle. He looked toward the kitchen. Leslie was absorbed in conversation. He opened one of the envelopes.

Please join us to celebrate the high school graduation of Justin Zacharias Chase.

Leslie snatched the invitation from his hand.

"Dammit. You weren't supposed to see that."

"What the hell is this?"

"Believe me, Richard, I wanted to send you an invitation. The truth is, he overruled me. He said he wouldn't show up if you were coming."

"He *overruled* you? My own son's graduation party, and I'm not even invited? Why?"

"I don't know. I just can't figure you two out."

Richard shook his head. "No, no, there's got to be something else. Leslie, he came to see me in jail. We actually talked. I know we've got issues, but this doesn't make any sense. Is he ashamed of his jailbird father? Is that it?"

Leslie lowered her head. "I'm afraid he overheard me talking to Adriana about, well, the roses."

"What? Leslie, how could you?"

"I'm sorry, Richard, I was so angry. I didn't think Justin was in the house. I had to talk to somebody."

"Why not me? How dare you go around airing our dirty laundry to your friends? I can't believe this. He hates me again, for something I didn't even do. I've been banned from my own son's graduation. Thanks a lot, Leslie!"

"What the hell did you want me to do? You think this is easy for me? You think I enjoy this internal love-hate battle I have for you raging inside me? You think I enjoy watching our only son reject his father? Look at me, all dressed up fancy, like I'm going on a date. But inside, I'm so twisted up. I can't decide whether to take you back or just walk away from you and this great big mess."

She headed for the stairs. "I'm sorry, Richard. I think it's best if you leave."

He watched her leap up the steps, head for their bedroom, and slam the door. He tentatively placed a foot on the lowest step and looked up.

"You didn't even tell me about your great news." He waited, but the door didn't open. He sighed and stepped back.

On his way out, Richard glanced again at that wonderful painting of the three of them. He stuffed an invitation into his pocket, scribbled a few words on the back of another invitation, set it on the coffee table, and quietly left.

44

The next morning, Richard opened his bedroom window and stared into the gray sky. He still wore yesterday's clothes. What did it matter? He had nowhere to go. He pulled the invitation out of his pocket, glanced at the photograph of Justin hanging on the wall, and made a call.

"Les, I'm really sorry for my outburst last night. Please give me a chance to sit down and talk to you, for just a few minutes." He waited. "Les, I—"

"I'm sorry too, Richard. I shouldn't have thrown you out like that. I do want to see you, but, well, just not now, at least not until after the party."

"My own son's graduation party and I'm not even invited? It's not right, Les."

"I know, Richard, but it's got to be his decision. I can't force him. What will that accomplish?"

"Maybe if you talk to him again."

"I will. No guarantees, but I'll do my best. I hope it works out, but if not, I'll call you soon. I promise."

"Thanks Les. Thanks for trying. Good night."

Richard ate little, drank too much, slept poorly, walked miles and miles, and tried to understand. He bought a small used car, for no other reason than to pass the time. He couldn't even speak to Charles, who was on vacation.

Leslie had promised to talk to Justin. That would have to do.

Two agonizing weeks crawled by without a call. The party was now only a week away. After a couple of glasses of wine, Richard called his son. No answer. He left a voicemail.

"Hey Jus, it's your dad. I know you're upset, but I'd like to talk to you. I'd like to see you, actually. Please give me a call."

The day before the party, he tried again. Again, no answer.

The morning of the party, he dragged himself out of bed after a fitful sleep of terrifying dream fragments of car crashes and crying children. He felt exhausted, more tired than when he had gone to bed four hours earlier.

His eyes fell upon the full-length mirror on the closet door. He looked at the man staring back at him—dark circles under bloodshot eyes; unshaven, greasy hair in all directions. Pale, wrinkled, beaten down. He rested his elbows on his thighs and stared at the crinkled invitation on the wooden floor between his feet.

Justin's rejection over the years had always tormented Richard, hovering over him like a black cloud. How much from that terrible afternoon years ago had Justin seen or heard? Maybe nothing at all. Perhaps teenage angst, or a response to a father too busy with his work over the years explained his son's behavior. On the other hand . . . Richard cringed at the thought.

Before his descent into madness—before the obsession with Lundh and the accident—Richard had always hoped that reaching out to his son with friendship and love would bring Justin around. He clung to that hope for a long time, even after his fall from grace. But now, in the time it took to reread an invitation through bloodshot eyes, he finally accepted the truth. The conversation Justin had apparently overheard about the roses may have triggered this latest rejection, but he knew in his heart that a much deeper conflict lay at the root of all this. The time for waiting and hoping for some painless magical resolution was over. If he wanted to get his son back, they would have to sit down together and talk it all out until they got to the bottom of everything, fully, openly, and honestly.

The idea frightened the life out of him. As a physician interested in the history of medicine, Richard had sometimes tried to imagine the fear and mental anguish of a patient with appendicitis or a perforated gallbladder going into surgery with minimal or no anesthesia. Richard's anguish was different, of course, but for the first time in his life, he felt at least some of that "no turning back, this could hurt like hell" feeling.

Did he want his son back?

Yes.

He would talk to Justin.

He pulled the invitation out of his pocket and read it again. He flashed back to when he first saw it at his house, stacked in a thick pile on the fireplace mantle. Invitations for everyone, it seemed, except him. A strange mix of sorrow and anger once again filled him, tightening his jaw. For a brief moment, he considered crashing the party, demanding to see his son, shoving him into a chair, and finally ending this horrible standoff, come what may.

The thought sickened him. What would that accomplish, other than ruin the party and drive his son further away? Sure, Richard felt hurt and angry and a part of him felt such an urge to lash out at his son with rage and righteous indignation, even if it all was rooted in love. But at the end of the day, no matter what the circumstances, what good did blind anger ever accomplish, even if a person felt they had been wronged?

He thought of Lundh.

No, not this time. Never again.

Richard opened his window and breathed in the cool morning air. How did he feel? He wasn't sure. The decision to reach out to Justin did seem to make him feel lighter, less burdened. But if the cloud of indecision and uncertainty had been pushed away, a new cloud, potentially far more ominous, took its place. He was clear about one thing. The sooner they did this, the better. He would contact Justin this coming week, through Leslie, if necessary.

He glanced at the invitation. How he wished he could congratulate his son on his graduation. But how? He could try to call him, but Justin hadn't answered his last several calls. Why should today be different? He slammed the window shut and sighed. He would just have to leave a voicemail. If only he could somehow—

Richard checked his watch. He had better hurry. He suddenly had a lot to do.

45

That evening, Richard slowly approached his house. Cars lined both sides of the road. Had they invited the whole county? He parked five houses away from his own. He squeezed the wheel and took a deep breath. He felt as if his heart might jump out of his chest.

He checked his watch—ten o'clock. He looked into the back seat for the canvas bag that held his gift-wrapped present. Now it was time to wait. He hoped he wasn't making a catastrophic mistake.

At a little past twelve thirty, guests began to emerge from the house. By one fifteen, everybody had left. Ready or not, the time had come. He called Leslie's cell.

"Richard?"

"I'm down the street in my car. I've come to congratulate Justin and give him a gift."

"You're *what?* At this hour?"

"I'm sorry, Leslie, I don't want to cause a problem, but I need to do this. Please understand. I just want to see him for a moment."

"Richard, please. This isn't the time—"

"He's my son, for God sake! I promise I won't make a scene. I just want to congratulate him. That's it. Then I'll be gone. I promise."

Leslie said nothing.

"Les, please."

Richard waited, not knowing what else to say.

Leslie broke her silence with a loud sigh. "All right. Come in through the garage and wait there."

"Thank you, Les. I won't forget this."

Leslie met Richard with a scowl. She escorted him to his office, and then left immediately, slamming the door behind her. The smell of paint and cleaners hit his nose. He found himself in a room of easels, paints, and canvases in various degrees of completion. He could hardly believe the transformation. For the twelve years they had lived here, Leslie had virtually never entered this room. Now it was her private domain, the studio she had always wanted.

Several minutes later, the door flew open and slammed shut. Richard turned around. Justin stood in the doorway with Leslie. He glared at his father.

"What are you doing here?

Richard took a single step toward them. "I wanted to see you."

"I can't believe you just barged in here."

"Justin, I didn't—"

"Say what you need to say, then get out!"

Leslie grabbed two wooden chairs. "Here, sit down, the two of you."

Justin ignored her. "Don't bother. He won't be staying."

"Sit down with your father. Now!"

Justin flopped onto the chair. Richard sat on the edge of his seat, hands on his knees.

"Son, I'm sorry to show up like this. I wanted to congratulate you and give you this. He took the gift out of his canvas bag and held it out to Justin.

"Congratulations?" He slapped the gift out of Richard's hand, sending it crashing to the floor.

"You got some nerve congratulating me. When I was a kid, did you ever help me with my homework, even once? No, you were too busy. You were always too busy. Mom helped me. Who drove me around before I got my car? Who went to the parent-teacher conferences? Who went to my games? And now, you have the nerve to congratulate me as if you had something to do with it? I think you should leave now. And take your garbage with you."

Leslie stepped between them.

"Justin, that's no reason to reject your father."

Richard sidestepped Leslie. "It's okay, I'll go." He headed for the door, and then turned toward Justin. "Look at me, sneaking in my own house *after* my own son's graduation party. Why? To embarrass you? To punish you for not inviting me? If I wanted to do that, I'd have crashed the party and been out there whooping it up with the rest of them. No, I came here because I wanted to see the only two people in my life who mean anything to me, to say I'm ashamed of what I've done, and to say I'm sorry, more than you can know, for *all* of it."

Justin sneered. "The only two people in your life who mean anything to you? Boy, you've got some nerve saying that in front of Mom. Have you forgotten that bitch you sent the roses to? Oh, but wait a minute. You probably don't need forgiveness from her, do you?"

Richard stepped toward them. "They were *pink* roses. *Pink*, for *thank you*, not *red*, for *love*. She copied Lundh's house keys while I was at work. I sent her the roses to *thank* her, not to get in bed with her." He turned toward Leslie. "How many times have I sent you roses over the years? Twenty-five, at least? Have you ever received pink roses? Even once? Every Christmas I send my office manager a gift certificate and a dozen roses. Pink roses! You want to see the pictures? If you don't believe me, call our florist. Charlene keeps great records. Anyway, she'll remember the order for Cathy Wilcox. Two dozen pink roses on short notice got her hopping, especially when she had a store full of red roses."

He headed for the door. "I'll see myself out."

Justin jumped ahead of Richard and slammed the door shut. "You think this is just about that? A bunch of fucking roses? After what you've done? You're pathetic!"

A searing heat rushed into Richard's head. He raised his open hand, and then froze. Justin recoiled back and tripped, falling to his knees. Richard stood over him.

"I am *not* pathetic! I am your *father*, and you are my *son!*"

Leslie threw herself between them. "Stop it, please, just stop it!"

Justin jumped to his feet, his face beet-red, his eyes tear-filled.

"You really want to know why I can't stand the sight of you, for all these years? Maybe it has something to do with that *bitch* you had on the couch when Mom was out of town one day, just before Thanksgiving, my freshman year. Forget about that? You didn't know I was home, upstairs in my room, when you came in with her, did you?"

A jolt of electricity shot through Richard.

"There I was, shivering under the covers with a fever. I

thought somebody broke in. Then I heard your voice and some *woman's* voice, and it sure as hell wasn't Mom's. I peeked downstairs. You want to know what I saw? You and that bitch right on the couch in the family room. Wow! I couldn't believe my eyes. I ran back to my bedroom and hid under the covers. A second later, I heard you coming up the stairs. You barely made a sound but I heard you on the wooden floor. I could tell it was your step. Then my door creaked open, just a sliver. I think I stopped breathing. Then I heard you go back downstairs and leave. You remember that day, *Dad*? Well I've lived with that day for the last four years. I couldn't tell you. You'd have killed me. I wanted to tell Mom, but I didn't want to hurt her. So I just kept it inside, eating away."

Richard stood facing them, unable to pull his gaze away from his son's glare. Justin's words cut deeply into him, twisting and tightening his insides, evoking fresh images of that horrible day. Finally, the moment he had been privately dreading and hoping with all his heart to avoid, had arrived. The big ugly scab had finally been ripped off. The bullet he had been dodging for all this time had finally struck.

Richard looked down for a moment, and then up at Leslie. She stood next to the doorway, silent and still, her arms wrapped around her chest, her big eyes tear-filled, her lips pursed together, the lines on her face showing her quiet sorrow.

Richard stepped toward his wife. "Les, I'm so sorry. I wanted to tell you, but—"

Leslie turned away from him. "I think it's time you left," she said, barely above a whisper.

Richard picked up his bag and slowly headed for the door, and then stopped and turned toward them.

"I wish with all my heart and soul that I could undo the past—the woman, Lundh, the little girl, *everything*. A day doesn't go by I don't regret all of it. Sitting in jail, I didn't know how I was going to get through it. I wasn't even sure I wanted to get through it. But then, when I thought it couldn't get any worse, I got lucky. I met some people, some great people. They made me realize that, despite all the terrible things I've done, my life is still worth fighting for. From that moment, everything changed. I didn't want to give up any more. I wanted to begin again, to try to make some kind of worthwhile life for myself and for my family. *That's* why I came here."

Justin stared at the floor, stone-faced. Leslie buried her face in her hands and sobbed.

"I'll see myself out." Richard said quietly.

He gently closed the office door behind him.

———

Leslie wiped her eyes.

"Mom, aren't you, I mean, you don't seem shocked or anything."

Leslie turned away. "I already knew about her."

"What?"

"Your dad and I were having a rough time. I knew something was wrong. He finally broke down and told me about the affair just before Christmas that year."

"He told you about that day, about seeing me?"

"No."

"I . . . I had no idea you knew."

Leslie turned toward her son. "Come here, sweetheart."

She hugged him. "My God, Justin. All this time. Why didn't you say something?"

"I told you, I didn't want to hurt you."

"If only we had known."

"You really believe his story? You know, about the roses and all that?"

"I don't know. Maybe I do. I just don't know."

She picked up the gift lying on the floor next to the chair and handed it to him.

"Go on, open it."

The old model airplane took Justin's breath away. He touched the broken wings and cringed.

"Mom, I haven't seen this in years."

Leslie smiled. "Me, neither. I think he had it in his office at the front desk. Remember, you two made it in the hospital when you were sick? You guys worked on that thing every night. You'd fall asleep with the plans in your hands. We figured building that plane with your dad did you more good than any medicine. That's when you said you wanted to be an engineer."

Justin rested the airplane in his lap and looked down. Tears filled his eyes.

Leslie took his hand. "Listen, sweetheart, I want to tell you something. I know we both have a lot of anger inside. To be honest, I really don't know what's going to happen. But I do know one thing. He loves you, Justin. He knew something hadn't been right between you two for the longest time. It's been eating away at him."

"Yeah, but that doesn't change what he did, does it?"

"No, it doesn't. But sometimes you've got to let go of the past."

"What about you?"

Leslie lowered her head. "I'm trying."

The office door flew open. Leslie's brother stood before them, panting. He smelled of beer.

"Boy, did I give that son of a bitch a run for his money. Told him if he ever showed his face here again, I'd personally come and kick his ass clear across the street."

Leslie ran into the hall. "What the hell have you done?"

"I see him leaving. He gets to the road, turns around, and starts coming back. So I cut him off. Says he left his keys inside. I tell him, 'Get the hell outta here. Go on, start walking.'"

Leslie grabbed his arm. "Have you got blood on your elbow?"

"Don't worry, it's not mine. Bastard wouldn't listen. Tried to get past me. I wouldn't let him, so the son of a bitch came at me. I caught him just above the eye."

Leslie threw her hands up. "Have you lost your mind?"

"Don't give me that shit. He deserved it. Right, Justin?"

Justin lowered his head.

Leslie peered out the window. "So where is he now?"

"I told him to wait in the street; I'd throw his keys out on the road."

Leslie bolted out the front door. A moment later, she returned to Justin, who was still holding the broken airplane.

"I can't find him," she said breathlessly. "He's not in the front yard or on the road."

She ran into the studio office and emerged with Richard's keys. "I'm going to look for him with the car. He can't be far."

Justin stood up. "I'll go."

"Let me come with you."

"No. I want to do this alone."

—⧓—

Justin drove up and down the streets of his neighborhood, unable to think straight. Using his high beams, he finally caught sight of his father just outside the gates, walking down the side of the road. Justin approached to within three car lengths behind him, turned onto the gravel shoulder, and stopped.

He slammed his fist down onto the horn, producing a loud, steady howl. Richard spun around toward him. Justin hesitated, and then stepped out of the vehicle. For a moment, they stood facing each other, silent and still, Justin in the shadows, his father silhouetted by the headlights. He wanted to walk toward his dad, but his legs wouldn't move. Anger and indignation seemed to cement his feet to the loose gravel. Yet he also felt another force thrusting him forward. After taking a deep breath, he willed himself to take that first step. When he looked up, his father was already next to him.

Justin glanced at the cut above his right eye and the dried blood on his cheek. "How's the eye feel?"

"Okay, I guess."

Justin tossed the keys to him. "Here. You're going to need these."

"Thanks."

"Looks like you need some stitches."

"I'm okay."

"Come on. I'll take you to the hospital."

They drove in silence. Justin sat still as a stone behind the wheel, self-conscious of every movement, even his breathing.

The short drive felt like an eternity. His father looked so thin. New lines had appeared everywhere on his gaunt face. Prison must not have been easy. He thought of all those calls and texts his father had sent him. He thought of those letters from prison. They weren't much, just a few words about prison life and how he missed his family and how sorry he was for what had happened. Justin now wished he had answered them, even if in anger. Heading for the hospital, he felt awkward saying nothing, but couldn't get his mouth to open, even for small talk. He wished his father said something, anything, but he remained silent. Justin tried to think of what had just happened and how he felt, but his mind couldn't hold on to a single coherent thought. He focused on the road and stepped on the gas.

The nurse estimated a one-hour wait. Justin stepped outside and phoned his mother. "I found him walking along Barkley. He's got a nasty cut above his right eye. We're at the emergency room to get him some stitches. I'll be home soon."

He flipped his cell phone closed before his mother could respond.

The waiting room bustled with patients. Justin and Richard sat next to each other in silence, watching the small, wall-mounted television in the corner. Forty-five minutes later, a nurse's aide called Richard's name.

As his father left the room, Justin stared at the floor. The time bomb had finally exploded. The burden he had been carrying now felt lighter, if just a little. So, where was that feeling of justice, now that he'd finally had his say? He shook his head and covered his face in his hands. Before, he had clarity. His anger was pure; his mind was clear. Now, what did he have? He picked up a car magazine and looked at the pictures.

Richard emerged from the emergency room with a white bandage above his right eye.

Justin stood up. "How does it feel?"

"Okay."

They walked to the car in silence.

"Can I drop you off at your house, you know, so you don't have to drive? You can get your car in the morning."

"Okay. Thank you."

When they arrived, Richard reached for the handle of the car door and turned to his son. "Back there on the road, did you think of running me over?"

For an instant, Justin imagined stomping on the accelerator, sideswiping his father, and seeing him lying on the side of the road, gravel sticking to his sweaty, grimacing face, waiting to die. A rush of nausea came over him. Tears filled his eyes. "Of course not."

Richard smiled. "A couple of months ago, I wished you would have. But not now."

Justin clutched the top of the steering wheel with both hands and looked straight ahead, barely able to see.

"Thanks for the drive. I'd better let you go."

Justin nodded, avoiding his father's gaze.

"Son, please look at me."

He turned toward his father. Richard extended his hand. Justin hesitated, looked into his eyes, and then did what he thought he'd never again do.

He shook his hand.

Tears rolled down his father's cheeks.

Justin had never seen his dad cry.

All at once, the terrible, black burden of resentment and anger that had lived with him for so long evaporated.

Richard stepped out of the car and was gone.

Justin drove home, parked in the garage, and went to the living room. His mother sat in a rocking chair before him.

"Eight stitches. I took him home."

"Did you guys talk?"

Justin's eyes filled with tears. He turned away.

Leslie hugged him. "Do you want to talk about it?"

"No."

She held him by the shoulders and looked directly into his eyes. "You sure?"

Justin nodded. "Yeah, at least for now."

———✵———

Leslie went upstairs into her bedroom. She pulled the crumpled invitation from her pocket and read Richard's words on the back.

Please forgive me.

She wiped her tears and got into bed.

Two weeks later, while eating his breakfast, Richard turned to the editorial page in the *Boston Globe* and was surprised to see his letter to the editor titled, "Backup Safety Features Could Save Lives." He smiled halfheartedly and set the page aside to share with Charles.

The editorial page on the following day published no less than six responses to his letter. They were generally supportive, but there was one that especially stood out—the tragic story of a couple who, after ten years of heartbreaking infertility, finally experienced the miracle of a healthy baby boy. The toddler broke loose from a babysitter and was run over with their car while backing out of the driveway. Richard's eyes filled with tears.

That afternoon, Leslie called.

"Congratulations on the article."

"Les! It's good to hear from you."

"Look, I was wondering, you could probably use a decent meal. You want to come over for dinner Saturday? Justin wants to tell you all about his trip."

"Yes, of course. I'd love to."

Richard tossed the phone onto the bed and jumped two feet high.

The next day, the *Globe* ran an editorial urging legislators to mandate car backup safety equipment, referencing Richard's letter and statistics. Along with the editorial, they ran more comments from letters, faxes, and e-mails from people describing their own stories of death, injuries, and near misses. Out of nowhere, a wave of suffering had fallen at his feet. The accident data he had been sent from the lady in Itasca suddenly felt real.

By the following afternoon, he had contracted a Web designer to create a site dedicated to safety issues for vehicles of all kinds—from bicycles to boats and all categories of cars. He posted crash-test ratings and the other research he had accumulated.

Buoyed by the response his letter had achieved, Richard called *Consumer Reports* magazine. Would they be interested in receiving a comprehensive article on rear-bumper detection devices? Yes, they would be happy to consider such an article.

The next morning, he headed off to the public library. He sat at his usual desk on the third floor next to a big window that looked out over a small courtyard. Leaves rustled in the maple trees. Puffy white clouds streaked across the bright-blue sky. He marveled at the fresh growth springing from the treetops. Such a wondrous renewal.

He began his work in earnest. He knew his efforts were not the kind that would generate widespread interest, but that was okay. If he could touch the lives of even just a few, that would be worthwhile.

After a day of research, Richard rewarded himself with dinner at one of his favorite Italian restaurants. The pasta primavera and Merlot were excellent. He looked at the couples and families around him and smiled weakly.

He reached into his jacket pocket and pulled out Justin's letter from Amsterdam, where he had gone to visit his best friend the day after the party. Since receiving it a week ago, Richard had read his son's letter several times a day, virtually memorizing it. Justin talked about his trip and his excitement over the engineering program at the University of Florida in Gainesville, home of the Gators. He missed his girlfriend. He would keep in touch.

My son has sent me a letter.

He tucked it back into his pocket.

Richard arrived home at ten o'clock and flopped into bed, exhausted. He fell asleep within a few minutes.

At a little after midnight, his cell phone rang, shattering his fragmented dream state. As he answered the phone, he noticed a recent missed call and a voicemail.

"Hello."

"Hello, Richard? It's Lewis Marcoux."

Richard sat up. He groped for his watch on the bedside table. "Marcoux? Is everything okay?"

"Yes, everything is fine. Listen, I've got some great news for you. We're having Leslie's showing tonight."

Richard threw off his sheets and jumped out of bed. "Tonight? I thought—"

"Sorry, I had to move it up a couple of weeks. Anyway, what a great night! I'm telling you, this stuff is the finest surreal work I've seen in the last twenty years. She doesn't know how good she is."

Richard paced within his tiny room. "So what's happening? Did a lot of people show up? What are they saying?"

"The place is packed with Chicago's finest. What are they saying? They're spending lots of money. That's what they're saying."

"You mean people are . . . buying her paintings?"

"You're damned right they're buying them, at least her best ones, as fast as I could show them, and for top dollar, I'm pleased to add."

"That's . . . wonderful! How much did she sell?"

"So far, about twenty-eight grand. I'll have to check."

Richard froze in his tracks. "Twenty-eight thousand?" He stared into space, dumbfounded. "Oh my God, she must be ecstatic."

"I just saw her. She's in shock. She looks as if she just won the lottery. You sure you don't want me to say anything about your involvement?"

"No! Absolutely not. You're not talking to me. You've *never* talked to me."

"Okay, okay, as you wish. I'll tell you, Richard, I don't see this every day. I mean, you wanting to stay behind the scenes like this, not grab some of the credit. You're a hell of a guy to do this."

"I didn't do a damned thing, Lewis. She did this all on her own. She just needed somebody to take a serious look at her work. She needed a break."

"And you helped make that happen."

"No, Lewis, *you* helped make that happen. I thank you more than I can say. Just promise me you won't say a thing."

"I'll take the secret to my grave. Hey, I better get going.

I just wanted to give you a call to let you know how it went." When Marcoux had finished, Richard tossed his phone onto the bed, looked at himself in the mirror, and shook his fist in triumph. He flung open his window and thrust his head outside. The cool night air felt glorious. He closed his eyes and imagined Leslie's joy. How wonderful and satisfied she must have felt. Just wait until Justin heard about his mom. What a special moment that would be.

He wished he could congratulate her now, tonight, in person. He yearned to tell her this was long overdue and well deserved. How he would have loved to be standing next to her and Justin, sharing in the joy of her accomplishment.

He looked into the night sky.

Please forgive me, Les.

He flopped onto bed, wide-awake, ripples of excitement coursing through his body. His elbow found his cell phone, knocking it onto the hardwood floor. He remembered the missed call and reached for the phone. The caller had left a voicemail.

"Hey, it's Les. You'll never guess where I am. I'm at the famous Marcoux Gallery in Chicago. I finally got my big break! My paintings are flying off the walls. I'm so excited I can barely breathe. I can't wait to tell you all about it tomorrow night. Justin and I are looking forward to seeing you. I'm not supposed to tell you, but you know that model plane you gave him? Well, he patched it up. You should have seen him. He glued every little piece back together. He's not saying anything, but I think he's really excited for you to see it. I better—"

Richard shut his eyes. He saw Leslie's face. He heard her voice. He imagined her loving touch. He thought of that grand moment in the car with his only son, tears streaming down their faces, shaking hands.

Oh, that magnificent handshake.

Maybe a new beginning. Something to hope for. Richard shook his head in happy amazement. Amid an avalanche of pain and suffering that he knew would never completely go away, he had somehow found some small measure of joy and hope—enough to keep him going, enough to make his life worthwhile.

He quietly celebrated.

Better get some sleep.

Tomorrow he was going out for dinner.

THE END

About the Author

Dr. Gary McCarragher was born in Montreal, Canada. He received his medical training at McGill University and enjoyed a successful career as a gastroenterologist in the Tampa Bay area before becoming a hospice physician in 2009. As part of his passionate advocacy for hospice care, Gary has a website dedicated to hospice and has published numerous articles on palliative care. Visit Gary's website at www.garymccarragher.com.

Gary also enjoys the arts, music, and performing in community theater, where he received an award for Best Actor. He is a member of the Land O' Lakes Book Club. He currently lives in the Tampa Bay area.

Unhinged is his first published novel.

CPSIA information can be obtained
at www.ICGtesting.com
Printed in the USA
BVHW082045140120
569366BV00002B/43/P